ELE FOUNTAIN

PUSHKIN CHILDREN'S

For T, with love

Pushkin Press
71–75 Shelton Street
London WC2H 9JQ

Copyright © Ele Fountain 2020

Lost was first published in Great Britain by Pushkin Press in 2020

1 3 5 7 9 8 6 4 2

ISBN 13: 978-1-78269-255-3

Designed and typeset by Tetragon, London
Printed and bound by CPI Group (UK) Ltd, Croydon, CR0 4YY

www.pushkinpress.com

Contents

You can't cross the sea
merely by standing and staring at the water

RABINDRANATH TAGORE

Street

I sense that I am being watched. I lift my head and see a station guard looking straight back at me. They don't normally bother patrolling the far end of the platforms. His hands are by his sides, but the baton he clutches tilts upwards, ready.

Our eyes lock, and my heart beats faster. I hold his gaze, while slowly unfolding my crossed legs. A low rumble grows as a passenger train pulls in. Its brakes screech and the guard's eyes flick towards the noise. In that split second, I push myself up and start to run.

He lunges to grab me but gets the edge of my T-shirt. I stumble but keep running. Behind me I hear his footsteps slapping on the hard floor.

"Little rat!" he shouts.

He is fat but fast. I weave round the concrete columns in the middle of the platform. His wheezing breath is loud and I know that he is close. There are passengers ahead, with bags strewn around. I leap over a large bag and swerve round a family. They shout at me to "watch out, rat".

I cannot hear the guard's footsteps now, or his raspy breath. He has decided to let me go.

Sweat runs down my back. The air is sticky, like always before the monsoon clouds burst, spilling soft rain on the city. I walk into the swelling crowd of passengers. People flow around me without making eye contact.

I crouch down next to a column of rusty, battered trunks, painted cream and blue like the trains. From here I can see the platforms stretching away in rows. On my other side is the ticket hall. A queue snakes from the ticket window. The customers cling on to wallets, suitcases, children's hands. They all have places to go, people waiting to see them. I was one of them. Now I have nothing. I am nothing.

I look across the platforms and see friends smiling and hugging each other. I see families chatting and sharing food. My stomach growls. I see men in suits, foreheads shiny in the sticky midday heat. But I am not really looking at them. I am looking for someone else.

I am looking for my brother.

Home

I wake to silence. Weird. As my confusion grows, the veil of sleep lifts gently from my senses, and I hear a soft thrumming sound which had muffled all others. Rain. Seconds later a bicycle bell tinkles below my window, then another, and from further away the unbroken song-like notes of a man praying. Monsoon! Finally. It's late this year.

I pull my sheet over my shoulders and lie in bed listening to the morning orchestra with its new percussion. Monsoon means watching films with Bella. It means hanging out with Amit. It means cooking with Mila. It means school holidays and new clothes. As I start to drift into a cosy monsoon daydream, my bedroom door swings open.

"Rain!" shouts Amit.

"Go away," I groan, my eyes still shut.

Amit stands in the middle of my room, wiggling his bottom from side to side and waving his arms in the air. "*Last week at school, last week at school,*" he sings, in an impressively high voice.

I tug my warm pillow from beneath my head and hurl it at him. "Do you know the words to the 'Go away I'm still in bed' song?"

I know grumpiness will have no effect on Amit. He is a puppy in a school uniform.

"Mila has made doughnuts."

"Doughnuts?" I sit up in bed. "When did Mila learn how to make doughnuts?"

"*I don't know, I don't know*!" Amit sings. Then before I can throw anything else at him, he runs out of my room and back to where the food smells are coming from.

I place my feet on the cool marble floor and follow the doughnut smell.

"Good afternoon." My dad looks up from some papers on the table, as I wander into the dining room. He's hilarious. "I'm sorry but we had to eat your doughnuts too. We were worried they might slow you down. I know you like to be ready first."

I look from the empty plate in the middle of the table to Amit's sugary, grinning mouth. "What! We've got loads of time. Haven't we?"

"We *never* have loads of time," Dad says, raising his eyebrows, "but I think you might be in luck."

Mila appears in the kitchen doorway, holding a small plateful of doughnuts. She carries it in front of her, like an offering from the enormous baby bump beneath, and places the plate on the table before I can intercept and help.

"Mila, your bump is even bigger than yesterday!" I say.

She smiles shyly. "Four weeks left now."

"What will we eat when you're not here?" Amit asks. "And who will tidy up after us?"

I find Amit's foot under the table and press down hard with my own.

"What was that for?" He frowns at me.

I look over at my dad, who looks down at his paperwork. He is in total denial about Mila leaving to start her own family.

She came to work for us after Mum died. Dad said he had to find someone fast, before Amit starved. Mila started on a trial, and eight years later she is still here. But not for much longer.

Mila says she has a friend who could take over from her. Someone she grew up with, someone trustworthy. Dad should snap her up, but there never seems to be a good time for Mila's friend to visit.

"I don't think they let you into school wearing bed-clothes," Dad says without looking up.

"Especially ones like yours," adds Amit.

I ignore them and sink my teeth into warm doughnut. Bella thinks it's weird that we all have breakfast together. Her dad is always having Breakfast Meetings or flying off somewhere, literally. It sounds like a good arrangement.

Outside a car horn honks, followed by three or four other honks and a man shouting. The rain will make the traffic worse than ever today. Too many millions of people on the city roads, which might be flooded.

"Delicious, Mila!" I shout in the direction of the kitchen.

"Not so loud," Dad scolds, half-heartedly.

Mila appears in the kitchen doorway again. She walks over to my father, moving silently, lightly, despite the extra weight she is carrying.

"Mr Morel, tonight would it be a problem if I left at six o'clock? It will take me a long time to reach home, I think, if the rain is like this all day."

"Of course," my father answers. "You must leave at six every night while the rain is heavy."

Mila always talks to my father like this. She's looked after us since we were tiny, but Mila isn't exactly *part* of our family. She works *for* our family. There's a big difference. Bella's always going on about the Big Difference, like I don't actually know. Bella also can't believe we

14

only have one person working in our house. She has six. Almost one for every day of the week.

Mila's pretty lucky though. She lives on the edge of town in one of the slum areas, but she gets to spend most of the daytime in our apartment, which is air-conditioned and huge. Dad says that when Mila leaves to have the baby, she will be one hundred per cent in the slum again, and that slums are no place to bring up a baby. I don't know why he cares particularly. Lots of people have babies in slums.

"Lola?"

"OK, OK, I'm getting dressed." Dad never shouts. *Lola?* is code red. Bella says her dad is always shouting, mostly at her mum. There's a lot about our family that I think Bella finds strange, compared to our other school friends anyway.

Despite having breakfast at different speeds, we all seem to arrive in the hallway to put our shoes on at exactly the same time. It's amazing how much three people can get in each other's way—especially in our new apartment, which is about twice the size of our old one.

I grab my bag and step towards the door.

"Lola." I hear Mila softly say my name. I turn round and she passes me a warm paper packet. I know there are two doughnuts inside.

Song

"Oh baby! Give me one more dance, one more dance, oh baaaaaby!"

Dad's head bobs from side to side as we sing at the top of our voices. But it's Amit who can hit all the high notes. Most of the time Amit is just annoying, but as soon as he starts to sing, something strange happens. It's almost like annoying Amit has been possessed by some kind of bewitching songbird. Then when he stops singing it's all about who's going to hold the TV remote again.

The car radio is turned right up. It feels as if the whole city has tuned in to the same song. I haven't seen the film it's from, but Bella and I have been practising the dance moves at lunchtime. Phones are not allowed at our school, but Bella always bends the rules. If someone complained, then her family could probably just buy the school—or at least buy someone

17

an enormous present, so they forgot that Bella had brought her phone in.

Rain hammers on the roof and cascades down the windscreen. The wipers can't keep up. We are in the middle of three wonky lanes of traffic. Nothing is moving. People press on their horns as if that will make any difference. While we're all singing, it doesn't seem to matter.

A man taps on the window and points to a basket of tissues and chewing gum covered in a sheet of plastic. His ragged clothes cling to him and rain runs down his face. He wants me to buy something. Through the car windscreen, he looks blurry, as if the rain has started to wash him away. I shake my head, annoyed that he's interrupted my song. The man turns to the car behind instead.

I remember my paper package and tap Amit on the shoulder. He stops singing and flashes me one of his megawatt smiles. His other special skill.

He takes a doughnut and pushes it into his mouth. Whole. I need to start documenting this kind of behaviour so that when he's a famous movie star I can embarrass him instead.

Last year Amit moved to a new school, one which specializes in performing arts. He has normal lessons as well as extra music ones, especially singing. At least he gets to wear blue. My uniform is a shade of green which doesn't exist anywhere else. Nature would never create a colour so awful or with so many pleats.

I tap him on the shoulder again. "When's your audition?"

"Next week. I've got to practise practise practise this week, and then give my voice a rest for a few days. My singing teacher thinks I'll get a part. Maybe not a big one, but she thinks that's better for my first film." He pushes his hands from side to side in a seat dance.

"Don't forget I'm coming to watch, OK?"

"Sure. As long as you don't embarrass me."

The irony is, he doesn't even know what irony means.

"Well it's going to be the holidays by then, so you should be grateful I'm not busy."

He rolls his eyes.

"I might ask Bella to come too."

"You don't have to go *everywhere* with Bella."

"I don't," I say, prickling. "She said she wanted to come. She's movie obsessed."

"OK, fine, she can come," he says, like he has just done me a huge favour, but I can tell that he's actually quite pleased. He starts humming. Even his humming sounds good.

Bella

"Sorry I'm late, Mr Banik. The roads were flooded."

He nods. "Sit down and open your book at page fifty-eight."

Bella looks up at me and rolls her big eyes. I am always late. My school is in the new part of the city. So are my friends. Dad will never move from the old town. He likes the narrow streets and little shops. I like shopping malls, ice-cream shops and not having to drive for an hour and a half to get to school.

I slide into my chair next to Bella.

"Look at my hair," Bella whispers.

I open my book at page fifty-eight and try to look like I'm reading it. "What about it?" I whisper back, hoping for a clue.

"The gold?" she says urgently.

I glance at the side of her head. Within her ponytail I can see strands of gold woven into the long black hair.

"Totally awesome," I whisper. Bella seems satisfied.

I have learnt how to listen to the teacher and keep Bella happy at the same time. *Totally Awesome*, *No Way* and *Yesss!* work for most things. I can listen to the teacher and nod to Bella. She talks a lot. But this time the teacher notices me peering round the back of Bella's head.

"Have you lost something, Lola?"

"No, Mr Banik."

Even though Mr Banik is still looking at us, Bella starts writing in the margin of her textbook.

When the teacher looks away, I glance down. She has written *Holiday Plans* in swirly writing, and a picture of a mobile phone with wavy lines coming out of it. She knows I don't have a mobile phone.

"Yesss!" I whisper. For the next hour and ten minutes while I am learning all there is to know about glaciation, Bella will be thinking about cool new shops for us to visit.

When the bell sounds for lunchtime, I drift towards the canteen. It's still quite empty so I spread my stuff out over a table in the corner and wave at Bella when she joins the food queue. She always schedules a hair-maintenance break before lunch.

"So, I have some ideas for next week," she starts talking before she's even reached the table. "How about a makeover party on Saturday? It would be such a great way to start the holidays." She doesn't even wait for a reply. "Who shall we invite?"

"Sounds fun," I say, "but I don't really have any make-up I can bring."

"So what? Mum bought bags of it at the airport last month and she doesn't even like most of it, so we'll have loads to share."

"Cool!" I say, and I mean it. Dad doesn't like me wearing make-up, so I only get to try things out at Bella's house. "Oh, and I asked Amit about his audition. He says it's fine if I bring you too. You might have to pretend you're my sister though."

"Woah that is sooo amazing!" Bella squeals, leaning forward to grin in my face.

I look up as Asha and Yasmin slide their trays onto the table to join us. "What's going on?" Yasmin smiles.

"Lola's brother is having a film audition and we're going to watch," says Bella.

"Do you think they might need some extras?" asks Yasmin, wide-eyed.

"I don't know; they're very fussy about who comes along to the audition," Bella says, like she arranged it all herself. "But we were thinking of having a makeover party on Saturday. Wanna come?"

"Yesss!" Yasmin and Asha say together.

Bella turns and looks appraisingly at my face, like I might be the focus of Saturday's makeover. "You have such great skin," she says. "I want to try some of my new highlighter on your cheeks." She reaches for a lock of hair from my ponytail. "I wish I had hair like yours, it's so shiny. You must brush it for hours."

I smile and nod, thinking how I brushed it for around ten seconds this morning.

I'm grateful when Asha says dramatically, "It's the boy with the green eyes. Twelve o'clock. Don't all look at once."

"Is he the one with the really cheap watch?" says Bella dismissively.

I glance at her face to see if she's joking, but she's not. Sometimes I try to remember how we ended up being friends. I pass under most people's radars. Not Bella's though. When we started having classes together, she seemed to pick me out, which felt good. The other girls don't invite me to after-school stuff because I live on the far side of town.

Bella liked the fact that I was usually free and I liked feeling included. Recently, though, it seems a bit more like I'm Bella's show-and-tell object, which is the same as being the odd one out again.

Unfair

Rain pounds on the car roof. We are stuck in four lanes of honking traffic again. This time, travelling in the other direction. Home.

"There's something in the boot I want to show you when we get home," says Dad.

"Is it a body?" asks Amit.

"It's new fabric. I'm thinking of expanding the factory." Dad glances at me in the rear-view mirror. "School skirts and tunics."

Amit rolls his eyes. "I would prefer a body."

"Lola, I'd like you to have a look."

"As long as it's not green like mine," I shout over the rain. "Can I go to Bella's house on Saturday?"

"What about me?" says Amit.

"We can do stuff on Sunday. Unless you want a makeover?"

"Who else will be there?" asks Dad.

Dad's never actually said he doesn't like Bella, but his voice changes when I talk about her. He knows she doesn't get good grades at school, and the school we go to is one of the best in the city.

"Just a couple of girls—Yasmin and Asha, me and Bella."

"OK, but you will have to take a taxi. I am going to visit a new supplier at the weekend. It's a long drive and the rains are bad, so I'll have to stay overnight."

"So I'm going to be on my own?" says Amit.

"Mila will be staying. You can invite a friend over if you want."

"I don't have time to make friends at my school. When it's not lessons it's singing, and when I'm not singing, it's traffic," Amit moans.

"Well, the holiday will fix that. You can get some rest, then you will be ready for your new term. It will feel new again for everyone then, not just you. That's the best time to make friends."

"Dad, when am I going to get a mobile phone?" I ask. "All my friends have one." We have this conversation every couple of months.

"You see plenty of your friends as it is, without having to spend every waking hour on the phone to them too."

"Then can we move to the other side of the city? There's nothing to do here, and it's so far from everyone. And everything," I add for maximum effect.

"Our new apartment has everything we need. It's not far from everything. There are plenty of shops and restaurants."

"Not any good ones."

Dad is silent for a second and I wonder if I've pushed it too far.

"I know the traffic is a problem," says Dad. "But houses on the other side of town are not value for money. You pay extra just to say that you live there."

"Well everyone else's parents don't seem to mind."

"Well I'm not everyone else's parents," Dad says.

"But—"

"That's enough, thank you, Lola."

I slump back in my seat. It's not fair. Dad says only little kids argue about fairness. Grown-ups try to find solutions. Maybe I'm not ready to stop being a little kid yet.

Mila

As we walk through the front door, I know something is wrong.

There is a faint smell of burning.

"Mila?" Dad shouts.

"Mila!" I shout more loudly. I kick off my shoes and rush towards the kitchen.

Mila is kneeling on the floor, her hand against the wall. Smoke billows from a frying pan of onion and spice.

Dad rushes silently to the hob and turns it off, then crouches next to Mila.

"What happened? Talk to me," he says gently.

Mila blows air slowly through her lips. She is staring at the floor, her face covered in a sheen of sweat.

"I think the baby is coming early," she manages to whisper, before slowly breathing out again.

"We must take you to a hospital," says Dad. "Lola, get some water for Mila."

"I can't see her water bottle," I reply. Mila doesn't share our plates and cups and knives and forks, even though Dad says she can.

"Lola, a glass. Now!"

"Home," whispers Mila.

"Hospital. I will pay. I will call your husband. He can tell your mother-in-law." I've never seen Dad speak sternly to Mila. "Can you walk?"

Mila nods. Gently, we help her to stand.

"What's happened to Mila?" Amit's voice wavers. He is pressed up against the kitchen wall, watching wide-eyed.

"Mila is in labour. She'll be OK. Amit, find her bag."

Slowly, slowly, we help Mila through the door and to the lift, which goes down to the underground parking space.

"Amit, you sit in the front with me. Lola, you sit in the back and hold Mila's hand."

Silently we follow our instructions. Even Amit doesn't complain about getting back in the car.

The last time Dad went to hospital was when Amit was born. Dad came home with Amit, but without my mother. I'm glad I don't remember anything about it. He says that Mum would have died whatever happened, but in a hospital at least they could save Amit.

*

30

Three hours have passed since we first came home from school. Two of those were spent driving to hospital and back in the rain. One of them was spent at home afterwards, trying to plug the gaps left by Mila.

"When can we call her?" asks Amit. His face is pale.

"Babies arrive in their own time," says Dad, putting his arm round Amit's shoulder. We are clearing up together, after a dinner made of leftovers from the fridge. "We'll call in the morning."

"But how do we know she's OK?"

"She's in the best place. Those doctors have delivered thousands of babies. Her mother-in-law is there too, to look after her."

Amit seems younger since Mila has been gone. I guess Mila has always been a part of his life, and none of us were expecting her to leave it tonight.

"I still have to visit the supplier on Saturday, but I will try not to stay overnight," Dad says.

"Who's going to do all the house stuff now?" Amit asks. This time I don't squash his foot.

"We'll manage for the rest of this week, and I'll find someone to start next week. Even if it's only someone temporary."

"What about Mila's friend?" I ask.

"Good idea," says Dad. I'm not sure he's properly listening.

31

Even though I know Mila is in hospital having a baby, it feels a bit like she's abandoned us.

I look over at Amit. Tears shine in his eyes. He wipes them away before Dad notices.

"I am going to make breakfast tomorrow morning," I announce. "Flatbread-egg sandwiches. How hard can it be?"

"Maybe you should start now," says Dad, "if you're going to be ready on time."

Amit can't help a little smile. "Can I have two?" he asks.

"Two for you, and none for you." I point at Dad.

The next day I am epically late for school.

"Lola, I have to know," says Miss Roy, my biology teacher, as I try to creep to my seat. "What is it that you have for breakfast, which takes so long to eat?"

There is a murmur of laughter around the classroom.

"Our housekeeper had a baby last night, Miss."

"At your house?!" she pretends to be shocked.

"No, Miss, but the baby came early so we weren't prepared."

"OK. Well I suppose that's a fairly good excuse."

"Thank you, Miss." I can tell that Bella is totally bursting to ask me what happened, but even she can see that I have to make up for some lost time.

At break time her squeals travel down the corridor as we walk along together. "A baby boy! Soooo cute!" Then her face falls. "She didn't actually have it in your *house*, did she?"

"No, we had time to drive her to the hospital."

"Wait, you drove her to the hospital? Wow, Lola, it's almost like she employs you, not the other way round." Bella raises one perfectly manicured hand in the air then lets it drop as if it, too, despairs. "It's probably good that you're going to get someone new. I'll ask Mum if you can borrow one of ours for now."

"Thanks, but I think Dad has someone in mind. A friend of Mila's."

"She'll be expecting the same treatment. I bet Mila has told her your dad is a soft touch."

"Dad's not a soft touch," I say to her back as she disappears into the washroom.

"Does he have a name?" Yasmin asks, minutes later, when Bella joins us in the playground and tells everyone about the baby. I put my water cup down.

"I don't know anything else apart from that it's a boy."

Asha nods, then says, "When our cleaner came back after having a baby, Mum caught her stealing milk powder from the kitchen." Bella gasps. "She said she couldn't afford to buy it and she couldn't feed the baby herself because she had come back to work. Mum said it sounded like she'd be better off not having a job at all then.

"Apparently the cleaner started sobbing, saying then she wouldn't be able to feed her family."

"Unbelievable," Bella says.

"So ungrateful," I add, when they all turn to look at me. My cheeks burn. I don't know if it's because I'm embarrassed by the attention, or ashamed of what I've just said.

Holiday

I wake to the steady thrum of rain falling. Again. I'm about to get out of bed when I remember I don't need to. It's Saturday. It's also the first day of the holidays. I reach for my book and lie back down to read. Bliss.

The last few days of school took for ever. Actually, without Mila to sort things out, everything seems to take twice as long. I'm running out of clean clothes and we've been getting takeaways from a restaurant round the corner every night. The food is OK but it's not the same as having it cooked at home. No second helpings for a start.

"See you tonight. Look after each other," Dad shouts from the hall.

I scramble out of bed. "Where are you going?" I ask, watching as he slips on his shoes.

"To see my fabric supplier. Remember?"

I hadn't. Dad kisses me on the top of my head, and ruffles Amit's hair. I think he's been watching too many family movies. "I've left taxi money and a bit extra for emergencies. It's next to the television."

"Have a good journey. Don't buy any green fabric!" I shout as Dad walks out of the front door towards the lift.

"Bring me something back!" Amit shouts.

"He's only going for the day."

"Well he always brings you something," Amit says grumpily.

It's true. Dad always brings me back a chain of marigold flowers when he goes away. Even if it's just for the day. He's been doing it since I can remember. Marigolds were Mum's favourite flower.

"Can you help me?" I ask. Amit's expression changes to curiosity. "What should I wear for Bella's, later?"

"Not clothes *again*," he groans.

"Not clothes?"

"I think you should wear clothes," he adds, looking horrified. "I just don't care which ones."

I know Bella will care.

"Don't forget to bring your music stuff. We can be your first proper audience," I say.

Amit looks happier. I felt sorry for him, having to spend the first day of the holidays on his own, so yesterday I asked Bella if Amit could come along and watch a film or something, while we do make-up stuff.

She grabbed my hands and said, *"Do you think he'll do his audition routine for us? We could critique."*

Amit said absolutely no way, but I know he won't be able to resist showing off a bit.

I check the time. "Oh no! Her driver's going to be here in ten minutes. Quick!" Bella wouldn't hear of us catching a taxi.

"I'm ready," says Amit. "You're the one who needs clothes, remember?"

The intercom buzzes just as I zip up my black jeans. There is no time to put my hair up, but then that's the point of a makeover. Although I know Bella will already be looking perfect.

After an hour we cross the flyover that separates the district near my school, where most of my friends live, from the rest of the city. We turn off and drive down a few smaller streets, then stop outside a large white building. Amit stares through the car window as the gate glides open and we drive in. Bella doesn't live in an apartment. She has a whole three-storey house.

The huge front door swings open.

"You're here!" Bella stands in the doorway beckoning to us. "I'm so glad you came too," she says to Amit.

Amit looks at her with a mixture of awe and apprehension. I realize that his expression probably mirrors mine.

*

I shouldn't have worried about being the main focus of the makeover. Bella, Asha and Yasmin are totally mesmerized by Amit's singing and dancing. They insist on giving him an *"audition styling"*, which he complains about, but I notice he sits very still while they apply black eyeliner. He spends a long time looking in the mirror afterwards.

They don't get round to doing my face until it's nearly time to go. We are actually *leaving* Bella's house when Amit reminds me that Dad will not be impressed with my gold eyeshadow and thick black eyeliner. It takes another twenty minutes and eight pieces of cotton wool to remove it all.

Lucky

We arrive home super late. It's already dark.

Amit knocks on the apartment door. When no one comes, I realize we are in luck. Dad must still be on his way back. I take the key from my pocket and unlock the door.

As I feel around on the wall for a switch, it takes me a second to remember why we are in darkness and no warm cooking smells drift from the kitchen. After the noise and buzz of Bella's house, the apartment feels strange without Mila.

I flick the lights on. Amit stands in the hallway, like he's forgotten how to move. I take the food containers from his hands. Bella insisted on loading us up with goodies now that we have No Staff.

"Take your shoes off," I call, as I put the food in the kitchen and wander over to the television control. Noises from the hall tell me that Amit has come back to life.

It switches on to News 24. There is a story about farmers and rice crops. Next it flicks to an aerial shot of houses which have become islands surrounded by tea-coloured water. Normal stuff for rainy season.

I flick over to the movie channel and leave it on for Amit while I heat up the food.

We eat in front of the television with the volume up extra loud, singing along to all the songs, even though we don't know the words to most of them. Halfway through there is a kissing scene and Amit runs into the kitchen making retching noises.

Dad never lets us have floor picnics. It's the perfect way to end the first day of the holidays.

I start watching a second film when I realize that Amit isn't singing along any more. I turn and see that his eyes are closed, his head resting sideways on the edge of the sofa. I tidy up the stuff from dinner then give his leg a gentle kick.

"Come on, sleepy head."

Amit opens his eyes and squints, looking round the sitting room.

"Where's Dad?"

"Maybe he had to stay the night after all. He won't be impressed if we're asleep in front of the TV when he gets back."

Freedom

I open my wardrobe and stare inside. A reassuring laundry smell wafts over me. So many clothes are squashed beneath the hanging rail, they're not really *hanging* at all. I tug a clean T-shirt from the shelf.

As I turn to find my jeans, a car horn sounds right outside my window. I rush over and peer down. Two men are talking loudly on the street outside.

Amit wanders into my room.

"Dad's not back yet," he says.

"OK," I yawn. I want Amit to get out of my bedroom, but instead hear myself saying, "I'll make extra egg flatbreads. He'll be hungry when he gets here."

"I'll help," says Amit. "If you can do it, then it must be pretty easy."

"It's hard actually, I just make it look easy. Get out the flour from the cupboard by the fridge."

I get dressed and wander into the kitchen. "How are you already covered in flour?"

41

Amit stands up holding a blue paper bag. There's a dusty white patch on his chest. "Someone left the packet open yesterday." He tilts his head to one side and raises his eyebrows.

"OK, OK. But assistants don't normally talk back, so put that down and get the frying pan."

Amit sighs but goes to look for a frying pan.

I try to imagine my friends making their own breakfasts. Perhaps it is a good job we live so far away and I end up visiting them, not the other way round.

At lunchtime there is still no sign of Dad. Usually if he spends the night away for work, Mila is with us, and Dad calls her if he knows he's going to be late.

I realize, with a little buzz of excitement, that this will be a really good argument for me having a mobile phone.

"What shall we eat?" asks Amit.

"Hmm... we have Dad's flatbreads and we can eat the rest of Bella's food."

Amit perks up. "Can I finish the chicken?"

"If you load the dishwasher."

"Deal. When do you think Dad will be back?"

"Definitely by dinner time. But more likely in the next five minutes," I tease, "so you'd better finish up that chicken or else he'll want to share it!"

After lunch Amit disappears to his room. There is a sudden burst of music, then the song changes and as the new one begins, I hear Amit join in. It's almost impossible to tell his voice apart from the artist's.

"Turn it down!" I shout, but only because that's what Dad would have said. I like it loud.

I sit on the bed and spread out my fingers, turning them to make the silver nail polish sparkle in the daylight. It's the only clue to my day at Bella's. Dad will make me take the polish off my fingernails straight away. He probably won't notice my toes for a couple of days.

There's also the huge ketchup stain on Amit's T-shirt from the "best burger and fries *ever*", made by Bella's cook. Normally Mila would deal with things like that, but Amit's seeing if leaving his T-shirt in a screwed-up heap on the floor will miraculously have the same effect. Once thing's for sure, I'm not going to wash it.

I look at my bookshelf and pull out a book I haven't read for a while. I make a soft nest from my pillows and sheet and settle down to read. There's no homework or school to interrupt, just Amit wailing high notes in the background.

After a couple of hours, the traffic noises are louder. I guess it must be rush hour, although it's usually more like don't-rush hour, because you're going to be sat in traffic for twice that long anyway. I go to the sitting room and open up the balcony door. A wave of warm, damp air washes over me. Rain drips from the edge of the balcony above, making a dark line along the pale floor tiles.

I step outside and peer over the balcony rail to see if any cars are waiting to drive into the underground car park. Nothing. A raindrop splashes on the back of my neck.

I wander back inside and close the door. Amit is in the sitting room.

"Any sign of Dad?" he asks.

"No, I just wanted to see if it was still raining."

"You could have looked out of the window. Why isn't he back yet?"

"I don't know. The news said there's been a lot of flooding. Maybe he got stuck somewhere." I feel a slight flutter in my stomach. Amit does have a point. Dad is never very late home. Well, never more than an hour or so. He's never been a whole day late.

I switch on the TV and flick to News 24. They're talking about pollution. I flick through to find another news channel. There is a woman talking about crops being damaged by the rain and about how bad the flooding has been in rural areas.

"Do you think he's OK?" Amit asks.

"I'm sure he's fine. Normally he'd just call Mila, but Mila's not here."

"I wish Mila were here," says Amit.

"Maybe we should use some of the money Dad left for a taxi and buy some dinner."

Amit looks interested. "Can we choose anything we want?"

"As long as it's not something stupid."

I am starting to feel like a mixture of Mila and Dad now. I want to feel like Lola again. I glance down at my fingernails.

"Don't let Dad see those," Amit grins, "he will go bananaramas!"

I smile. "He will definitely go bananaramas. OK, let's go."

"Yes! Dinner dinner dinner..." Amit starts doing his excited dance in the hallway.

We step outside and the warm air envelops my face. I smell woodsmoke and incense. There is also a delicious aroma of spices and food cooking.

"Chicken and rice," says Amit. "No, wait, burger!"

Round the corner from our apartment is the old city. The streets are narrow and wires criss-cross overhead—wires for telephones, electricity, internet. It's like a separate wire city above our heads. Back on the street, people criss-cross, funnelled between shops and storm drains.

I pull Amit to the side of the street to let a cycle rickshaw pass. There is the sound of chisels tapping on stone, rickshaw bells tinkling, shopkeepers shouting to each other. A man hurries past with an enormous woven disk on his head. On top of it are four chickens.

Dad tells me that Mum loved walking down these streets with me, chatting and buying things. I wish I could remember. My only memories of Mum are from when she sat on the floor next to my bed and sang while she stroked my hand, until my eyes began to close.

A few metres ahead, steam rises from a huge metal pan.

"I want some of that," says Amit.

"We're not buying street food, Amit. We'll go to the restaurant where Dad bought takeaway."

"But you said I could have anything I want."

"Anything you want—from there."

While I pay for our order, Amit wanders next door to the kite shop. It's easy to see what every shop sells, because once the shutters are pulled up, their insides spill out onto the streets, letting the shopkeepers reel you in like fish: *"new delivery today"*, *"come and try it"*, *"best quality"*.

"C'mon," I call, reeling him back out. "Let's go and eat it while it's hot."

Amit is instantly at my side. "Let me carry the bags," he offers.

After the noise and smells of the street, the apartment seems especially quiet, so we eat dinner watching TV.

Afterwards, Amit plays some games on the tablet. I find it hard to concentrate on reading.

Distraction

I wake and listen to the rain falling. Then I remember Dad. I throw off my sheets and go to his bedroom. The bed is empty.

An icy wave passes through my stomach.

Amit is still sleeping. I turn on the news, quietly. There are more reports of flooding. I listen carefully to what the newsreader is saying and run to find a scrap of paper and a pen. I write down the names of the districts which have been most affected. I switch on my computer and stare at a map.

Where did Dad say he was going? I wish I'd paid more attention. Most of his suppliers are in the big towns to the north or to the east. He said he should be able to drive there, have a meeting, then drive back in one day. How far does that mean he went? Three hours? Four hours? When the roads are bad it takes twice as long to get anywhere.

I type in our location and choose a town. The route planner says it will take four hours to get there. During rainy season that could mean eight hours. I pick somewhere a bit closer. Two hours and fifteen minutes. I choose six more towns a similar distance away and write down their names. Then I turn over the paper to see what the newsreader had said. More than half of my towns have been badly affected by the flooding.

I touch the keyboard but my hands are trembling. I hear a noise behind me and turn round. Amit is standing in the doorway.

"What are you doing?" he asks.

"I'm just checking what's on at the cinema."

"Is that a map?"

I close the lid of my computer.

"Is Dad in his room?" asks Amit.

"Dad isn't back yet," I answer, trying to keep my voice even. I turn to look at him again. He is motionless in the doorway.

"He's not back?" I see tears pooling at the bottom of his eyes.

I walk over and put my arm round his shoulder.

"Don't worry," I say, trying to copy the low voice Mila uses when we're upset. "I expect Dad decided that the flooding was too bad and it would be dangerous to drive. He's been sensible and stayed there for a bit longer."

"Why hasn't he called?"

I smile. "How would we know? Perhaps he has called. Perhaps he's called Mila, like he always does. I guess Dad isn't used to Mila being gone, just like we're not used to it."

Amit wipes his nose on the back of his hand. There are no more tears. I feel reassured by my explanation too. It seems reasonable.

"Dad really has to buy me a phone now."

"Me too," says Amit, sniffing.

"You're only eight," I reply, thinking how I've had to wait five years longer than that already.

"But what if you were out too?" he says, his voice wavery again.

"Perhaps you do need a phone as well. We'll tell Dad. We're going to have a new housekeeper next week anyway. You'll never have to eat my flatbreads again."

"I like your flatbreads," says Amit.

"Shall we get some breakfast?" I ask.

"And then can we go to the cinema?"

I look at him, confused. "Oh yes, the cinema!"

I have no idea what's showing today, but we both need to get out of the apartment.

An hour later, I open my umbrella and we squash underneath it. Rain thunders down on the canvas and splashes up from the pavement. People rush past in both directions, mostly soaking wet. We walk clumsily to the main road and wave down an auto rickshaw. We clamber in, trying to close the umbrella without getting soaked. The driver covers our legs with a plastic sheet and steers into the beeping, tinkling mess of cars and rickshaws.

It feels like we're doing something we shouldn't, even though I know Dad wouldn't mind us going round the corner to watch a film. I guess it's because we haven't been able to ask him first.

Amit looks at me and smiles. "This is cool. Way better than going to Bella's house."

I try to soak up Amit's excitement, instead of all the rainwater which has pooled on the plastic seats.

Denial

When we get home, I make hot chocolate. It mostly sticks to the bottom of the mugs, but still tastes good. We choose our favourite dance scenes from the film and try to recreate them. Amit is so good at stringing different moves together that I end up just watching him.

When the rain stops, we rush out to get food. We even eat to the rhythm of the rain now.

The next morning, I lie in bed listening to a rickshaw bell tinkling. As it gets louder then fades away down the street, a quieter noise takes over. The *drip-drip* of water from a drainpipe somewhere outside my window.

Inside the apartment, it is silent.

My bedsheet rustles as I push it away and swing my feet down to the floor. My bare feet patter on the hard tiles as I walk to Dad's bedroom. His bedsheet is still smooth and untouched. Before I can check to see if Amit is awake, the intercom buzzes.

Relief washes over me and I feel so silly about worrying why Dad was held up for a few days. I peep in to the sitting room to make sure there are no empty food containers lying around, then brush my hair away from my face.

I run to the hall and press the intercom buzzer.

"You're late!" I laugh. "Soooo late."

"Who is this?" a man answers, but it's not my dad.

I feel my heart begin to thump. "It's Lola," I answer.

"This is Mr Dewan. Is your father in?"

"He's not here right now, he's on a work trip," I answer. The man at the other end seems immediately more chatty.

"OK. He's been away? OK. Can you tell him Mr Dewan called. I work for Mr Nilsen the landlord for this building. When is he due back?"

"Today. I'll tell him as soon as he is back."

"OK."

Amit is waiting in the hall. He looks confused.

"Was that Dad? It didn't sound like him."

"I think it was someone who works for the landlord. That's what he said."

"Mr Berg? Why did he come here?"

"Not Mr Berg. Our new landlord."

54

Amit stands very still. "And you said Dad will be back today?"

"Maybe even this morning."

Amit starts singing, *"This morning, this morning, he'll be back this morning"*, dancing his way to the kitchen.

I don't feel hungry. I go to sit on my bed.

I wonder what Bella is doing now. She said something about family coming to stay. It feels like I could be a thousand miles away from her. There won't be any school for weeks. If I wish hard enough, I wonder if a phone will suddenly appear on my bed.

I put one foot on the smooth marble, then stop. If I message Bella on my laptop, she will want to switch the video on. Then I know Amit will walk by and somehow Bella will find out that Dad's not here. I don't want her to know that we are here alone, doing everything for ourselves.

Instead I pick up my book. I want to be somewhere else for a while.

My mouth feels dry, but later I manage to eat some breakfast.

"I want to play cricket with Nish," says Amit. Nish is a friend from his old school.

"I thought you said he wasn't around in the holidays. Who do you hang out with at your new school?" I ask.

"I told you. No one yet," he says.

I think for a moment. I want us to stick together, just until Dad is back with the car. "We could go bowling," I suggest. "Bowling's way more fun than cricket."

"Yesss," says Amit.

Amit doesn't seem to have heard the last bit. Cricket is way more fun than pretty much everything, according to him.

I check the pile of money next to the microwave. There's not as much as I thought. In the drawer under the TV is the emergency fund. If I put it all together then we probably have enough to go bowling and get dinner too if we need to. I'm not used to checking how much money we have. I normally just ask Dad for it.

The bowling alley is crowded with all the other kids who've just finished school for the holidays. There's a sort of party atmosphere which Amit plugs into. It's not like he needs extra energy.

What I find most annoying is that Amit is better than me at bowling. Even though he can barely lift the ball I choose, he insists on using one the same weight, and somehow propels it in a smooth, straight line towards the pins every time.

"Strike!" Amit punches the air, then turns to grin at me. I can't help grinning back. Especially as his mouth and lips have turned bright blue from his iced drink. It's a colour almost as unnatural as my green school skirt.

On our way home it starts to rain super hard. The rickshaw pulls up outside our building and we shout to the guard, so that he can open the gate before we step into the downpour. We run to the main doors, through the lobby and up the stairs. Neither of us wants to wait for the lift. Amit bangs on the front door. When no one comes, I hunt for the key, rain dripping from my hair and the end of my nose.

I open up. Inside, it's dark and quiet. No one is home.

"I'm going to change," says Amit quietly, and disappears to his room.

I go to my room too. I need to think. I count on my fingers.

Dad has been gone for four days.

I wish there was somebody in my family I could call. They all moved far away when I was little. Dad said they didn't approve of him marrying Mum, and if they didn't approve of her, then he didn't approve of them. It would be very helpful now, though, if everyone had approved of each other. Then I would have some relatives I could call, like a normal person.

Who else might know what to do? School is shut until after summer. I've been to Dad's factory a couple of times, but it's miles away in a suburb. I don't even know where. Plus, why would Dad go there and not here? My thoughts circle back to Bella. I decide to send her a quick message. Just to say hi. When she replies, then maybe I can tell her what's going on.

Bella doesn't message me straight back. I check my emails. Dad doesn't like computers. He is more of a face-to-face person, so I don't expect a message from him, but you never know.

There is nothing.

I close my laptop and wait.

Missing

The next morning when I wake up, for a split second I feel sleepy and calm. Then I remember Dad.

I sit up and swing my feet down to the cool floor. I don't have to go into his room to know he's not there. Dad's been gone so long he wouldn't just creep in and go to bed. He would come to find us. See that we were OK. Hug us and apologize for being away so long. He would give me a loop of marigold flowers, their orange blossoms threaded tightly together to make a soft, sweet-smelling chain. This time it wouldn't be one of the little ones, only the width of my hand, it would be a beautiful looping circle which I could hang from my door.

The intercom buzzes. I hear Amit's feet patter on the marble floor.

"Hello?" he says, his voice higher than usual. "Dad?"

"It's Mr Dewan. Is your father at home?"

I open my bedroom door and walk quietly towards Amit. He turns to me with big eyes.

I whisper, "Tell him Dad left early for work." I sense we shouldn't let the landlord know Dad hasn't been home.

"He's not here, he left early for work," Amit replies.

"OK. I will drop by to see him at work. If he calls, perhaps you could remind him that the rent is several weeks overdue."

"Yes. Bye," says Amit.

I close my eyes and press my fingertips to my forehead.

"Did I say something wrong?" Amit asks.

"No, no. It's fine. Let's just hope Dad gets back very soon."

"Does Dad owe somebody money?"

"Maybe Dad forgot to pay the rent to the new landlord before he left. He'll be able to sort it out as soon as he's home."

"Oh no!" Amit holds his hands in front of him. "What day is it?"

"Wednesday."

"I think my audition is today."

I stare at him. "Do you know where? Can you remember who it's with?"

Amit shakes his head. "They talked to school, and school talked to Dad."

60

Dad wouldn't miss Amit's audition. There is no way he wouldn't be here.

"I'm going to get some water," I hear myself saying. I walk over to the microwave and pick up the small pile of money. I can't believe we spent so much on bowling and snacks. I count out the notes. We have to save what's left for food. I'm not sure how to work out what we'll need.

I feel like there is something obvious we should be doing to find Dad. I want to go out and look for him. I want to do something useful, but I don't want to frighten Amit.

I rush back to my bedroom and open up my laptop. On the news are more pictures of houses surrounded by water, cars rolled onto their sides. Several reports say that a big section of highway was covered in water when a river burst its banks. Vehicles were washed away. I stare at one of the images of cars piled by the roadside. I am no longer looking at them as if they belong to someone I don't know. I am looking for a silver car. A coldness spreads through me as I spot silver car after silver car. None of them looks quite like ours, but I'm not completely sure.

I look up at my bedroom door and imagine Dad appearing in the empty space, walking over to me and giving me a hug. Asking how school was. His arms would be warm and he would smell of soap.

I jump when Amit appears in the doorway instead.

"What should we do?" he asks. "About my audition."

I beckon Amit over, to come and sit down next to me on the bed.

"I think we just have to wait. There's nothing else we can do. I'm sure Dad is OK. He's probably stranded. The roads are all flooded, so there must be lots of people trying to get back into the city. Maybe his phone got wet if he was waiting in the rain. It won't work if it's waterlogged."

Amit stares up at me, waiting for me to tell him more, to reassure him. I put my arm round his shoulder.

"I'm sure he's OK though. I'm sorry you can't go to your audition this time. You're so brilliant, I bet you get another one really soon."

Amit's eyes begin to shine with tears. "I don't care about the stupid audition. I want Dad to come home."

"I know. So do I."

But Dad doesn't come home the next day either. Or the next.

Police

On Saturday morning I am woken by the intercom buzzer. An angry voice is saying, "Hello, hello?"

I kick off my sheet and rush to the hall.

"Hello," I say. "Who is it?"

"It's Mr Dewan. I work for Mr Nilsen. I went to your father's factory, but he wasn't in his office. In fact there were only a couple of people there. They said your dad hasn't been in this week. No one wants to work if they won't get paid. May I come in and speak to your father? Mr Nilsen is worried about your rent payment. Perhaps if your dad can talk to me then everything will be OK."

"Dad is away on another work trip. I think maybe the roads are bad and it's taking him longer to get back."

"Have you spoken to him?"

"No."

"When you do, can you remind him that this is a luxury apartment. There are people waiting for apartments in this block. People who pay on time."

The intercom is silent.

I realize that my hands are shaking.

Amit hasn't come out of his room. I know he must be awake. He probably heard everything.

I open my laptop and check my messages. There are five from Bella. She has flown off to visit her aunt. The internet is slow. She's bored. Let's plan for when she's back next weekend. When is the audition? Can I let her know so that she can keep her diary clear.

I reply to say that I'm so sorry, but the film people have now said that Amit can only take one person to the audition. I'll let her know how it goes. If he gets the part, maybe she can come to the premiere instead.

Why don't I tell her what's happening? If she's not back until next weekend, then there's definitely no point. Anyway, if I say that Dad has disappeared and we're on our own in the flat, she will go bananaramas, when I'm trying to feel calm.

I know Bella will talk to our friends about nothing else for maybe the rest of the summer holidays. About how we coped, despite everything. I would rather sort things out, and then tell her my own version. Or maybe nothing.

I press down the handle to Amit's bedroom and step in. Amit isn't lying on his bed or listening to music or playing computer games. He is sitting at his desk staring out of the window.

"Amit," I try to make my voice sound cheerful. "We're OK. We still have some money left. I think we need to keep it for food, though. Just to make sure we have plenty to eat until Dad gets back."

"What if he never comes back?" says Amit without turning round, his voice barely louder than a whisper.

"Don't be silly. Of course he'll come back. And when he does, he will say how grown up we've been for looking after each other. The first thing we need to do today is go out and get something for breakfast, and maybe some fruit too. Come on. Get dressed. You'll feel better when you've eaten."

I pause.

"Amit, maybe we should go to the police station too."

He spins round to face me, wide-eyed.

"Just to see if they have any news about the floods, or people who might have been hurt. They might be able to tell us what we should do. Maybe other people will be there asking about their families. I'm sure we're not the only ones waiting for someone."

Amit gets up slowly, like his body is moving on auto-pilot. He slides his wardrobe door open. There are big gaps on the shelves which are normally stacked with the clean, ironed clothes, now rising up in a heap from the floor behind him.

I check the internet for the nearest police station then collect a handful of coins to buy food. Amit is waiting for me in the hall with his shoes on.

The police station isn't far. Outside a group of men are chatting. They stare at me and Amit as we walk through the open gate towards a small white building with peeling paint. Inside we wait beside a plastic table and chair. A man in a uniform of pale-green shirt and dark-blue trousers comes over.

"No kids," he says, sounding tired.

"We're here because my dad is missing," I say. I expect him to be concerned, to start taking notes.

Instead the man says, "Where did he go missing?" which seems like a strange question.

"He drove out of town on business seven days ago and he hasn't come back yet."

The man nods. "Where was he going?" he asks.

"I'm not sure," I answer, feeling stupid.

"What about your mother? Is she not looking for him?"

"My mother passed away," I say.

The man nods again. "How do you know he didn't just decide to stay away a bit longer?" he asks, like that would be a normal thing to do under the circumstances.

"He always calls if he's going to be late."

"OK, let me take his car registration and your phone number in case I have any news." The officer looks round the room as if he is expecting someone else to come in.

"I don't know the car registration, and I don't have a phone."

"May I have your name?" he asks.

I give him my name and Dad's name.

"Aren't you going to write them down?" I say.

"I'll write them down when I get back to my office," he says. "I'm sure he'll turn up in a few days." He turns and walks back down the corridor—slowly, not like someone who's rushing to write down our names.

I look at Amit. "Let's go and buy some food," I say.

We eat breakfast and watch television. I look at denim jackets on my laptop. Amit plays computer games. Our apartment feels large and echoey. Several times I am about to go and see Mila in the kitchen, when I remember she's not here either. Amit and I drift around like two ghosts.

When I lie in bed that night, I am grateful for the gentle pattering of the rain outside to send me to sleep. Tomorrow is Sunday, and for the first time ever, I want the weekend to be over. Monday is always a busy day for new orders at the factory. We will drift through tomorrow, and then maybe everything will be alright. Surely Dad can't be away for two Mondays in a row.

Fear

On Monday morning, I switch on the TV but nothing happens.

"My light bulb has gone," Amit shouts from his bedroom. I feel a thump in my chest. I flick on the light switch in the sitting room. Nothing happens. I run into the kitchen and try the microwave and the kettle. Nothing is working. We have no electricity.

I realize I am breathing quickly. I flip open my laptop. It's almost out of battery. I turn it off.

"Amit, is your tablet dead?" I ask, keeping my voice as level as I can.

"I don't know," he calls back, "I think there's a bit of battery."

"OK. Don't use it for now. You need to save it. I think the electricity is down."

He patters out of his bedroom, his tablet under his arm. "Do you think it's gone down everywhere? Do you think it's because of flooding?"

"It's happened before," I say. "Sometimes the power cables get washed away."

Before I finish talking, the intercom crackles into life.

"Mr Morel, this is Mr Dewan. We've been unable to contact you at home or in your office. No one seems to know where you are. I will let you have until tomorrow to pay your outstanding rent, after which I'm afraid I will need to take action."

I look down and see that Amit is clinging to me. I stroke the top of his head.

The intercom crackles again, then is silent.

"It's OK, he's gone now."

"Do you think…" Amit pauses. "Do you think Dad might be… dead?" he asks.

"No!" I say too loudly.

Amit starts to sniff.

"No," I repeat softly. "That's a silly thing to think. I don't think Dad is dead. I think he's trying to get back to us, but he can't. Amit, do you have any friends we could stay with for a few days? Until Dad is here and we have electricity again?"

"I told you I don't have any friends at school. None I could stay with, anyway. Why not Bella?"

"Yes, I'll ask Bella," I say, even though I know she won't be back until the weekend.

I open my laptop and stare at the dark screen. Switching it on will use precious battery, but I have to make a plan.

I power it up and start typing: *Can't wait for you to come back! Can we come over on Saturday? Amit needs someone to listen to his new song.*

She types back straight away. *Fly back Friday p.m. Shopping and song on Saturday?*

Shopping and song, Saturday, I reply.

I close my eyes, to clear my head. Perhaps the landlord thinks that Dad is at home with us, hiding. If he turns the electricity off and we still don't pay, then he'll know we're not going to.

I feel like the landlord has done this before.

I wish I could ask someone in my family for help. I feel a spark of anger that Dad didn't keep in touch with them. I should be able to call my uncles and aunts, or my grandparents. Dad said they were different people to us, and that now they've moved away, there's no point in meeting. But family is family. Bella is always going off to weddings and birthday parties of cousins and other relatives.

"What did she say?" asks Amit.

"Who? Oh, Bella said how about Saturday."

"And today is only Monday? So we have to stay here. What will the landlord people do when they come back?"

"We still have twenty-four hours—at least. If Dad comes back tonight, he'll be able to sort things out with the landlord straight away."

"But what if he doesn't come back tonight?"

"Then we wait to see what the landlord says."

"Can we go out somewhere today?"

I pause. "We have to keep enough money for food. There isn't much left, so I think we might need to hang out here." I remember the electricity. "Don't open the balcony door, Amit. The air con is off, so we need to keep the cool air inside."

I walk round the apartment, opening up the blinds to let in as much light as possible. I'm about to search for the TV remote when I remember there's no point. Next to the television is a cupboard with some pottery bowls on top. I know they must have been Mum's. Dad doesn't really care about ornaments, apart from the ones she collected. I pull open the cupboard doors. Inside are boxes of board games. There are word games and Battleships, Ludo and some packs of cards. I haven't played a board game for ages.

"Amit!" I call. He runs in looking worried, then his eyes flick from my face to the pile of games on the floor. "What shall we play?" I ask.

He puts a finger to his mouth.

"Don't spend too long choosing," I say. "I think we'll have a chance to try them all."

When I wake up, I cannot work out where I am. Something moves beside me, and I remember that I slept on Amit's floor last night. He didn't want to be alone.

There is a bang on the door. Amit sits up in bed and we look at each other, eyes wide. I walk quietly to the hall.

"Mr Morel," a voice says loudly.

Someone is standing only a few feet away. The big new front door, our barrier from the outside world, now seems like nothing more than it actually is—a thin piece of wood.

"Please open the door."

Amit and I stand motionless.

"OK. I am leaving an eviction notice." I hear something tap against the bottom of the door. "You have seven days to empty the property of your belongings."

I hear footsteps tap across the floor outside, then the lift doors sliding open.

Amit's shoulders begin to shake as he cries. I put my arms round him.

"Shh. It's OK," I whisper.

"It's not OK," says Amit, into my damp T-shirt.

Leave

We have a new routine. One which doesn't feature bags of shopping, food cooking in the kitchen, ironed clothes or cool, polished floors.

In the morning we open the windows. There is no point in keeping them shut any more. Any benefit from the air con has long gone. We open the balcony doors wide and eat outside, between kitchen bowls filled with landscapes of wax and tilting candles from the night before.

In the evenings I read to Amit out here. Evening time is when I feel Dad's absence the most. The noise from the city makes it better. A bit. At least other people are busy going to work or coming home or seeing friends, like normal.

Amit is becoming a master of Battleships and is pretty good at chequers too. When we get tired of playing, we lean out of the windows, looking for a silver car.

Looking for a man who might be our landlord. We don't tidy, but I persuade Amit to put some of his clothes back in the wardrobe, so he can reach his bed.

At mealtimes, we go out for food. The shopkeepers are paying us more attention. Some of them recognize us now. Amit has started saying hello, just like Dad.

There is no sign of him, no news—but people don't just disappear from the face of the earth. Someone must know where Dad is, somewhere. We have to be patient.

On Friday morning I decide to ask Bella if we can stay for a few days when we come on Saturday. I'll say that we have a problem which I'll explain when I see her. I switch my computer on and start typing. I can't seem to make it sound quite right.

While I am rewriting the message, my battery runs flat.

"I'm just popping out for a second!" I shout to Amit.

"Where?" He appears in the hallway before I've had a chance to slip my trainers on.

"I'm going to see if anyone is at home in the flat upstairs." I'm not sure what I will say. I've never seen the people who live there. Maybe I'll ask if their electricity is down too.

I walk across the landing to the stairwell. Amit watches me from our doorway. I pad up the steps to the landing above and tap softly on the door.

No one answers, so I tap again, harder.

Either our neighbours are at work, or they've heard what's going on, that we might be evicted.

I head back down, my thoughts racing. "No one there," I say to Amit, trying to sound calm. I walk back inside and sit on the sofa, staring through the big glass doors to the balcony. Now that I have no way of reaching Bella, I realize how much I wanted to.

Without the television or the internet, I feel like a new world war could break out and Amit and I would be the last to know.

The rain is soothing. It is reassuring. The rhythm is constant, and then at some point it always stops, and the street sounds get louder again.

On Monday night I lie down on the bed of cushions I've made on Amit's floor.

I pick up my book and open it at the folded page. I read until Amit falls asleep.

Just as I am about to blow out the candle, Amit says, "Do you think the landlord will come tomorrow?"

"He said seven days. So I guess that means tomorrow. Sleep now, we can worry about that in the morning."

I lie with my eyes open, hoping to hear the soft scrabble of a key in the front door as Dad lets himself in. The gentle thump as he places his work bag on the floor.

Eventually I must drift off to sleep, because I wake to the sound of hammering at the door.

"It's Mr Dewan. Please let me in."

I peep round the doorway of Amit's room, to the hall. Voices are murmuring on the other side of the front door.

"We will return in one hour with a key. Please ensure the property is empty and vacated," someone shouts through the door.

"We have to leave? We have to leave our home?" Amit whispers. He has joined me in the doorway. His face is pale and there are dark circles around his eyes.

I look at him, trying not to let panic take over.

"Find your school rucksack, Amit. Pack some clothes. Pack anything you don't want to leave behind, but make sure it's not too heavy."

I take my rucksack from the wardrobe. "Pack a sheet!" I shout. I fold mine and stuff it into the rucksack, with some clothes and two books. I look round my room at the posters, my desk covered in small boxes and jewellery. I pick up my two favourite necklaces and put them in the rucksack, then I push several bangles into the side pocket.

I go into Dad's room and gaze around. What would he want me to take? I open and shut his wardrobe, and stare at the clothes hanging neatly. The folded shirts. I grab one of Dad's T-shirts.

I rush to the sitting room. My eyes flick from the large lamps to the mirror, the bowls and vases that Mila would dust. Nothing to fit in a rucksack. Then I go back to Dad's room. Next to his bed is a photo of him with Mum. I slip it into my rucksack. Then I take it back out and remove the photo from its frame. I squeeze my eyes tightly shut and then fold the photo in half and put it in my pocket.

"Sorry Mum, sorry Dad," I whisper.

Amit walks into the room. "What else should I take?" he asks in a quiet voice.

"Let's go to the kitchen," I say. "We have to be quick. I don't want to be here when the landlord and the other men come back. They'll have a key. They can just let themselves in."

Amit looks at me, wide-eyed. "Quickly," he says, "we have to hurry."

We stand in the middle of the kitchen, staring at the sleeping appliances and cluttered worktop; the table where Mila prepared our meals.

"Bottles of water," I say. "One each."

"Maybe a bowl?" says Amit.

"What for?"

"Well, what are we going to eat out of?"

"We will find somewhere to stay, don't worry." I don't want to think about having nowhere proper to eat. "It's time to go." I walk into the hall to put my trainers on.

"Umbrella!" says Amit.

I take one of the little umbrellas hanging on the coat rack. Then I turn round for another look at the flat. I want to stand there for longer, but Amit is tugging on my hand.

"Lola, we have to get out before the men come."

We click the door shut behind us, and I put the key in my pocket, just in case we need it. I hear the whirr of the lift coming up.

"Let's go down the stairs," I suggest.

We put our rucksacks on our backs, and head towards the stairs, tapping down them two at a time.

"Stop," I whisper at the bottom. "Don't run, just walk normally." It doesn't feel right to run away from our own home.

There is no one in the lobby.

The gates open and we step out onto the street. As the gates close behind us, I feel Amit's hand slip inside mine.

The street looks different. Everyone seems to be hurrying somewhere. Out of habit, I turn left towards the narrow streets of the old town. Amit follows.

In my pocket is the last of the money. Two men bustle past with large bundles balanced on their heads.

A bell tinkles behind us and a rickshaw rattles past. I don't feel like a customer shopping any more. I feel in the way.

Each shop is surrounded by goods, stacked or piled, a shopkeeper nested within. People stop, then move on, looking for a good price. Smells from the food stalls waft down towards us.

"I'm hungry," says Amit. I have no appetite, but I know I should eat something.

I take a few coins from my pocket and buy a couple of flatbreads.

"Is that all?" asks Amit.

"We need to save money. It will fill you up."

"Where shall we eat them?"

"Let's eat as we walk along," I say. His hand slips from mine and we walk in silence, tearing off strips of warm bread.

"Where are we going?" Amit asks when he's finished.

I am still eating, which gives me more time to think of an answer.

"Can we go to Bella's? She said she'd be back on Saturday."

"It's a long way, and we don't have enough money for a rickshaw," I explain. It's also very far from our apartment, and Dad, when he comes back.

Amit is silent.

81

The air feels warm on my face. I look up and see low cloud, in billowy shades of grey. It's going to rain. We could shelter in a doorway, but the rain might not pass for a few hours.

The first few drops fall heavy and large. I put up the umbrella and Amit links his arm through mine, huddling against my side. Ahead—where the winding, narrow streets of the old town join the wide main road—is a large tree. Amit sees it too. Arm in arm we run, rucksacks shuffling up and down on our backs.

We duck under the wide canopy and lean against the trunk. It's quieter beneath the broad branches, and only occasional drops of water slide from the leaves.

I watch people running for cover, plastic bags over their hair; rickshaw drivers stop to unfold fabric roofs above their seats and passengers. Car horns beep as the traffic slows. Despite the rain, it feels as if the whole city has somewhere to go.

While Amit watches the cars, I realize the truth: that we have nowhere to go, and nowhere to be. My head spins.

Amit thinks I have a plan. Everything I've learnt, everything I know, feels useless now. I don't want to be the one making decisions, in case I make the wrong one, but we can't stay under this tree all day.

A movement in the corner of my vision makes me turn round. A boy is leaning against the railing—a street rat.

He's wearing a blue plastic poncho. He is staring at me and Amit. Perhaps he thinks we have some coins to give. I shake my head. As I lower my gaze, past his dark orange trousers, I see that he has no shoes. Somehow, though, his feet are clean, surrounded by puddles of mud, leaves and plastic bottle tops. My eyes slide back to his face. He's still staring, like we are some sort of puzzle to solve.

A car drives past and splashes muddy water up my legs. I wave my hand in the air, but I doubt the driver can see, as the roof and boot are piled high with luggage. This gives me an idea.

"Amit, when the rain is less heavy, let's go to the train station," I say.

He looks up at me in surprise. "Where are we going?"

There is a trace of excitement in his voice. Like I have somehow fixed things.

"We're not going anywhere." I ruffle his damp hair, where it flops over his eyes. It needs a cut. "But I think it might be a good place to keep out of the rain if it's going to be like this for hours."

A rickshaw rattles past, spinning up more spray. The other lanes of traffic creep slowly along. A man picks his way past the buses, cars and rickshaws, his feet disappearing beneath the rising water.

"OK," Amit says quietly, "but let's not wait until the rain is less heavy. Can we go now?"

As we step away from the tree, I turn to look at the boy, but he's vanished.

The station isn't far, but walking is slow. We pick our way between the traffic and the plastic-covered stalls at the side of the road.

Outside the station is a crush of vehicles delivering passengers. There is no orderly queue. They look like the cars on the news, like they've floated here and ended up in a messy jumble. People are shouting and honking their horns.

We squeeze through into the ticket hall, where wet travellers call out instructions to friends and family crowding round the ticket office. There's no queue here either, just bodies pushed together. Street rats tap people on the arms to see if they want help with bags.

Amit and I push through to one of the platforms. It is almost empty. The train must have just left. I see that here we fit in. We have backpacks. We look as wet and scruffy as everyone else who's just arrived.

It feels like we can pause here. Like I can think about what we must do next. I didn't realize how much of my day is normally arranged by other people. I never had to choose what to eat or, if it was a school day, even what to wear.

We sit in silence on one of the benches which encircle the concrete pillars on the platform.

Amit says, "How will we know when Dad is back?"

"What do you mean, how will we know?"

"I mean, now that we're not at home, we won't know when he comes back. He won't know where we are either," he adds.

"We'll go there in the morning. When Dad comes back and finds out that we aren't in the apartment any more, he'll wait there for us."

"Do you think he'll be cross with us?"

"I think he will be proud of us. He will be proud of us for looking after ourselves while he's been away."

"But won't he be cross about the apartment?"

"We stayed as long as we could, Amit. I'm sure they'll put our stuff somewhere and then we'll just have to look for a new apartment."

As I speak, a chill rushes through me. I hadn't thought about what would happen to our stuff. All my clothes, my books, Mum's pottery. If someone else starts renting our flat, they won't want our things there.

I blink away the tears which rise up without warning. I picture my little boxes covered in silk and gold thread. Inside are tiny folded notes from Bella, cinema tickets, a shell which Amit gave to me. Someone might be in my bedroom right now, going through my wardrobe. My sadness turns to anger, anger that the landlord didn't give us more time, so I push the thought away. I don't want Amit to ask me what's wrong. I know if he does I won't be able to stop my tears.

I take a few deep breaths, and say, "I think maybe we should stay here tonight."

"You mean, sleep here on a platform, like a street rat?" Amit looks at me in horror.

"We'll never be street rats, Amit," I say calmly, even though I don't feel calm. "It's dry here and we can find a quiet corner. There won't be so many people around later. We just need somewhere to sleep while we wait for Dad. If our landlord wasn't so greedy, we'd still be in our apartment. It's his fault. He wouldn't wait a few days longer for Dad.

"We've still got a little bit of money, but we'll have to be really careful that we don't spend too much. We have to make it last."

A man and a woman come and sit next to us on the bench. The woman smiles at me and then carries on talking to the man. They think we are here to catch a train, just like they are.

Slowly the platform fills with people.

"How old do you think he is?" I ask, pointing to a white-haired man with a small bundle in his arms.

"I think he's at least one hundred years old," says Amit.

"And how about her," I point to a girl a little bit older than me.

"Thirty," says Amit. I laugh. My face feels like it's making a brand-new shape. Like I've never laughed before.

"What do you think that man does for a job?" I point to a man standing in front of a large box.

"I think he collects monkeys," he says.

I smile. For a few days, I'd forgotten how much Amit makes me laugh.

When the passengers begin to melt away, we huddle under my umbrella and walk the short distance from the station to where all the food carts are, waiting for hungry travellers. We choose something and the man wraps it in paper for us.

We find an empty corner of the ticket hall and crouch down to eat. I think we might be OK here for a couple of days. By then Dad will have made it back to the city.

Night

As dusk falls, neon lights click on across the station. The ticket hall seemed overcrowded before, but now it feels too bright for the handful of people wandering through.

Amit leans his head on my shoulder. "Where do you think we should go to sleep?"

I look around. There are some metal luggage trunks stacked up along the side of one of the platforms. Behind them we would be out of sight and sheltered from the rain.

"Let's try over there," I suggest. Amit tags slowly behind. "This looks OK."

The floor is smooth and dry, and the lights aren't as bright here. Amit unzips his backpack and pulls out his sheet. I lay it on the floor and put my rucksack down as a pillow. Amit does the same at the other end. We lie top-to-toe, with the other sheet on top of us. Somehow that makes it feel more like going to bed. The floor tiles press against my knee and hip.

"I can't sleep," whispers Amit. "I keep thinking about the man banging on our door."

"He won't find us here," I whisper back.

After a few minutes have passed, I push myself up on my elbows and look over at Amit. He doesn't stir. His chest is moving steadily up and down. I lie on my side and listen to the clank and scrape of metal shutters being pulled down for the night. I hear footsteps clipping quickly across the echoey ticket hall. Rain patters on the ground just beyond the platform roof, and a car horn sounds.

I close my eyes and try to picture my bedroom; my wardrobe with a mirror on it, my desk covered in jewellery boxes and moisturizers and all my favourite things, my bookcase. Then my thoughts drift to Dad. At home, it felt like he might walk through the door any second. Here, he seems very far away.

I wake to the sound of scuffling.

"No!" shouts Amit.

I sit up and see two boys tugging Amit's rucksack from his arms. I lunge towards the nearest boy and push him. His friend gives one last tug and pulls the rucksack free, then starts to run.

"Give it back!" Amit is about to run after them but I pull him back.

They jump off the edge of the platform and disappear into the darkness.

Amit turns round. "Why did you stop me?" he yells. "All my things were in there. All my clothes, everything!"

I look towards the ticket hall and see two or three groups of boys half-hidden in the shadows, leaning against the walls. They are looking in our direction. I pull Amit behind the stack of trunks.

"Amit, I'm sorry," I whisper. "I didn't want you to run after the street rats. There were two of them, and only one of you."

"I could have caught them," he says angrily. He sits on the floor and starts to cry. I put my arm round him.

I hear voices talking softly. They seem to be getting closer. Maybe other rats want our stuff too. I tap Amit on the shoulder and put my finger on my lips. I wrap my sheet around my shoulders and gesture that he should do the same, then as silently as possible I pick up my rucksack and push it into a small gap at the end of the trunks and climb in behind it. I peer out and beckon to Amit.

Amit's anger has all gone. He looks at me with large frightened eyes, his face wet with tears. He can hear the voices now too. He squeezes in on top of me. He is completely still. The trunk handle digs into my knee and Amit's head pushes against my chin. The voices stop, close to where we were sleeping. If they see us, there is no way we will be able to run from our hiding place. We are trapped.

I hear them say something about a girl, then their voices fade as they move away, walking further down the platform.

"Don't move," I whisper to Amit. He doesn't answer, but a warm teardrop splashes softly on my arm. I squeeze him more tightly. Without turning my head, I can see that the sky outside is beginning to lighten. The rain has stopped too. I wonder when that happened.

After half an hour or so, there is the grating sound of shutters being pushed up. A woman calls out to her friend.

"I think it's OK to leave," I whisper.

"How do you know there aren't some rats waiting for us to come out? Waiting to steal your rucksack?"

"They must have thought we ran off down the tracks ages ago. People are starting to arrive at the station, and there'll be guards too. They wouldn't do anything now. Let's walk back home and see if Dad's there."

As I say the word *home*, I realize that I shouldn't call it that any more. How can it be our home if we're not allowed there? How can it be our home, without our things? Without us? But there is nothing to replace it, and I can't bear the feeling of nowhere being home. Home is a part of me, like my name, like my family. Something safe, something familiar.

I stuff the sheets into my rucksack and slide it onto my back. As we walk round the stack of trunks, I'm surprised to see how many people are on the platforms already, moving quietly as they position themselves for the first trains.

We walk towards the main entrance, past a man with a large pile of bags and suitcases. A street rat stacks them onto a trolley, then leans against the handle to make it move. The trolley is about four times as big as he is. He's wearing orange trousers. He looks at me. With a jolt, I realize it's the boy from yesterday. He's not wearing his blue plastic poncho now. He's wearing one of Amit's T-shirts.

I swallow and keep walking, without slowing down, hoping that Amit hasn't noticed. The boy recognized me though. He looked for just a fraction too long.

Lost

As we enter the old part of town, I hear the rhythmic *thump, thump* of drums. Incense wafts in the air, its sweet smoky smell catching at the back of my throat.

"Is it a festival?" Amit asks.

"I guess it must be. I don't know which one." I try to remember which day it is.

As we get closer to our street, we have to slow down behind a crowd of people softly singing, and carrying a large statue covered in gold paint and flowers. I strain to see round them, holding Amit's hand tightly as we push past. When we emerge on the other side, we'll be able to see our apartment.

I feel my heart flutter in my chest as I look up, but there is no familiar figure leaning against the wall, waiting. There is no one there at all. We press our faces against the bars and look across the courtyard. I wave at the guard but he shakes his head. He won't let us in. He knows who we are. He's opened the gate for us many times before. The landlord must have told him not to let us in. I feel the blood rush to my cheeks. The gate used to be there to keep people away from us. Now it keeps us out.

Amit peels his hands from the bars. "What should we do?" he says.

"Let's get some breakfast. I'm hungry," I lie.

We turn back towards the procession as it flows past carved doorways and crumbling walls, through the heart of the old town. We have no choice but to merge into the flow, if we want to reach the food stalls clustered further along.

Bodies jostle against us and I'm glad to have the protection of the rucksack on my back. We surge helplessly forwards, and I realize it will be impossible to stop and buy something to eat without being trampled. I look over at Amit, being gently engulfed by the unseeing crowd. Ahead I know there is a little alleyway off to the side. Perhaps we should wait in there until the procession has moved along a bit.

"Amit, follow me."

I step away from the slow-moving tide and into the narrow passage. I reach my hand out to him but he doesn't take it. As I turn back to the crowd a bolt of panic burns through my chest. Amit isn't behind me.

"Amit!" I shout, straining to hear a response above the drums. I grab the corner of a building and push myself up, higher than the sea of heads.

I shout his name again; people turn to look at me, but no one can stop. The slow flood is carrying them off, too.

I push back into the crowd and try to force my way forwards. A woman tells me to watch out as my rucksack knocks against her face. Another alleyway is coming up. I stare along the gloomy passage until the crowd pushes me on. Ahead is a junction with a bigger road. I step away from the procession and look around me at the groups of people watching. Amit isn't here. I think of him reaching out for my hand and realizing I've gone. Tears spring to my eyes. I let them fall until my face is wet and I feel them drip onto my T-shirt.

Why didn't I hold his hand in the crowd? How could I have been so stupid. Why didn't I check that he was following me?

Surely he will stay in the old town. He won't leave without me. He's never really gone anywhere alone.

A group of people walks past, singing and clapping. I look away and use my fingertips to wipe the tears from my eyes. I don't want to talk to anybody, but it feels like they can see straight into my head anyway, like they know I've lost my little brother; that it was my job to look after him and I didn't. I let him lose his rucksack, and now he has gone, too. How can Amit survive without me? How can I survive without Amit?

Alone

As daylight fades, the crowd begins to thin. Petals and flowerheads litter the streets but the smoky incense smell has gone.

I search street after street, every passage and alleyway, no matter how narrow. I return to our apartment. I ask in shops. As I describe Amit, I realize that he could be any eight-year-old boy. How could anyone pick him out from the hundreds of children walking down the street that day?

I hear my stomach growl. My feet ache, but they keep on moving. I cannot rest. Not without Amit. He is alone with no money. No one to hold his hand.

If he is walking up and down the streets like I am, there is a chance we will keep missing each other. I decide to stay in one place for a while. I choose a shop selling bright squares of fabric. Some are displayed on a large wooden box near the front. If I sit with my back to the box, and my feet in the street, I am in no one's way.

I take off my rucksack. My T-shirt sticks to my back, with no cool air to dry it. Dark grey clouds gather above, made darker still by dusk creeping across the sky. Warm yellow lights begin to flicker on up and down the street. I scan the face of every passing child. Some of them smile back at me. Others hold their hand out for change. Even though I don't have a home, to them I look like I have money to spare.

Food smells waft past me as people walk along holding steaming packets. I realize I haven't eaten all day. I'm not hungry, but I know that I must not go a whole day without food. I have no energy. Without eating, I can't look for Amit. I get up to buy some flatbread and chicken. My mouth is dry and all I can think about is whether Amit has something to eat too.

I begin to feel very sleepy, but I keep on looking at the faces of children passing by. Some shops slide their shutters down. The man who owns the fabric shop behind me takes the folded cloth from the top of the wooden box but doesn't tell me to move. Maybe he can't be bothered, now it's the end of the day. He doesn't seem to care whether I'm there or not. I almost wish he did. Piece by piece, I seem to be disappearing from the city. I feel my eyes start to droop.

My heart aches as I wonder what Amit is doing now. A man and a woman walk past. The woman is laughing. I want her to be quiet. It doesn't feel right that anyone should feel happy right now.

I wake with a start. The side of my head hurts where it's been resting against a wall. I can't believe I fell asleep. What if Amit has walked past and not seen me in the shadows? The street is quiet, except for the sound of running footsteps fading into the night.

Yellowish bulbs hang outside a few of the shuttered shops. The sky above is black. It must be two or three in the morning.

I shiver and turn to get a jumper from my rucksack but the step beside me is empty. My rucksack has gone.

I find it hard to feel upset. Losing some necklaces and bracelets and a few clothes doesn't seem important after losing Amit. I shiver as I think of someone creeping up to take it, without me even waking. I slip my hand into my back pocket and touch the photo of Mum and Dad. I don't want to look at it right now.

I hear voices getting closer. A couple of men talking. I lean back into my shadowy corner and press myself against the wall, trying to stop my chest from heaving up and down. The men walk past, laughing and gesturing.

They don't look my way, but I know it's only a matter of time before someone does.

I wait until the only sound is the buzzing light bulb hanging opposite, then I walk a little further down the street until I find an alleyway. I am about to step into the gloom when a movement makes me freeze. As my eyes adjust to the darkness, I see that there are already two people sleeping here. They are wrapped in sheets. I can't tell if they are men or women. As silently as I can, I turn round and head back to the shop.

I hope Amit has found somewhere to spend the night. If I am scared, how must he feel?

Freefall

As the sky slowly lightens, there is a regular swishing sound. A street cleaner sweeps bits of food into a small pile. Shopkeepers push their shutters up and start arranging baskets and boxes outside their shops. A man stops right in front of where I am sitting.

"This is my shop," he says. He takes a key from his pocket and bends down to the padlock at the bottom of his shutter. "You can't stay here." He doesn't seem angry, but he doesn't look at me while he says it. He just expects me to leave.

"I'm looking for my brother," I say.

"Well he's not here, is he?" the man answers.

I want to tell him that I fell asleep here by accident. That my dad owns a factory. My dad's factory is probably a hundred times bigger than this shop.

I stand up and brush down my jeans, then I walk away down the street. On top of a flat trolley, a man heats up oil in a huge battered saucepan, while stirring something in a bowl.

I peer into every small space and corner, hoping to see Amit's face peering back at me. As I get closer to our apartment, I try to suppress a wave of excitement, only looking up at the last minute. The pavement is empty. I walk up to the gate and put my head against the bars. The building is silent. The windows stare blankly. My excitement swings to a different feeling, one that I don't recognize. I feel lost.

I feel like I'm in a car with no brakes. I don't know how to get back in control, how to stop.

Where do I go now?

I cannot face another day of searching the old town. I stand on the pavement for a few minutes, my back to the apartment building. The train station is the only other place Amit knows how to get to on foot. I will go there.

The walk to the station seems further than before. My legs feel weak. Outside the ticket hall is the same mess of taxis and rickshaws, horns honking, bells ringing, people shouting. It's the same place as yesterday, but I am different.

People stare at me. As I walk past two women chatting, one of them reaches out to touch my long hair, like I'm a goat or a sheep to buy. I brush her hand away.

But she has already turned to carry on talking to her friend. I have no rucksack to show that I have places to go to, somewhere to be. I have no little brother to show that I'm not alone.

My stomach aches with hunger. Everybody seems to be eating—reaching their hands into paper bags or small plastic packets, folding up flatbreads with fried egg inside. I realize that now I am staring too.

A picture of Mila comes into my head. Mila standing in the kitchen stirring pots that hiss or bellow steam, spreading warm spicy smells around the kitchen. Turning to smile at me and point to a plate of something on the kitchen table. Something warm and sugary. I picture Amit running in to grab some food then rushing off laughing. A wave of guilt smothers my hunger.

I scan the crowds of people, looking for a small, frightened face, then walk slowly round the edge of the ticket hall. Street rats wait here, looking for someone who needs help with their luggage. They stare at me, like they are trying to work out what kind of passenger I might be, with no bags and no company. They don't suspect that I am homeless too.

I walk to the platform where Amit and I slept. The metal trunks are still there, but that is all.

There are shouts from outside the station. I look through the entrance door and see that it's started to rain hard. A drumming sound begins on the roof, metres above my head.

I wander along the other platforms, checking behind the pillars until I see one with a group of boys halfway down. They see me coming and start calling out. They ask if I want to go and hang out with them. They want to know if they can touch my beautiful hair. I turn round and walk back the way I came, my cheeks burning. It feels like everyone has seen me; everyone except Amit.

The sun sinks lower in the sky. I feel dizzy with hunger, but I cannot rest. Whenever I sit down, or lean against the wall, I feel eyes upon me. My own eyes ache from looking, searching. Some of the street rats who've been here since I arrived begin drifting away from the ticket hall. Night-time waits like a dark hole. I can't go back to the old town. There will be nowhere dry there, nowhere safe.

I walk the length of a platform again, just to keep moving. I look up, and see a shape in the twilight, which I didn't notice before. In the distance, far down the sidings, just before the train tracks all loop round to the right, are a couple of old train carriages. They melt into the plants growing up from the tracks around them. They are the same grey-blue as the sky.

My hunger has turned into a calm feeling. It feels a little bit as if I am floating along the platform, rather than walking. I want to close my eyes and wake to find that the last few weeks were nothing but a nightmare. That I'm in my bed, in my apartment, with Dad and Amit sleeping just next door, and school tomorrow with my friends.

I think of Bella and am thankful that she never travels anywhere by train, only car or aeroplane. What would she think if she could see me now? My clothes dirty, my hair unbrushed. I haven't bothered to look in a mirror for almost a week.

I look around me. There is a handful of passengers scattered along the platforms. The overhead lights have switched on, and beyond the platform the tracks are slowly disappearing into dusk. I jump soundlessly onto the track, and head towards the old carriages, picking my way through the bushes at the edge as rain soaks through my T-shirt.

When I am level with the first one, I see how rusted and ancient it is. I don't look inside, but keep going to the very end, until I am as far from the station as possible, and completely out of sight. I try the handle of the final carriage but it's locked. The windows have grills across them. I look all around on both sides, but there is no way in.

My arms and legs ache as if I've been running. Water drips from my hair and down my face. In desperation,

I crawl underneath the carriage for some shelter. The gravel digs into my hands and knees and the ground is covered in a layer of sooty dirt. I cannot sit up, but for the first time in three days, I feel as if no one is watching me.

I twist round and look along the underbelly of the train. A metre or so from my head, there is a hole in the metal, just bigger than a dinner plate. Pale dusk light filters through the hole from the carriage above. Had it been any later, I wouldn't have seen it at all.

I turn and crawl towards it for a closer look. The edges are rough, but not sharp. If I can squeeze myself through the gap, then I will be inside the train. It will be dry, and I will be able to stand up. It must be cleaner than the gravel I am lying in. It's awkward to pull myself from lying to sitting, but I manage to push my head through the hole, then shuffle my shoulders up, and use my arms to haul my legs in.

The light is fading fast, but other than a pile of rags or sheets in the corner, the carriage is empty. It's like a tiny room. My room. A feeling of relief bubbles up inside me; almost immediately it disappears, as I picture Amit sheltering from the rain in a doorway or wandering along a street, hungry and alone. There is space to stretch out in the carriage, but I curl up in a corner.

I have lost all the things I care about, and I don't know how to get them back.

My only connection with Dad and Amit is the apartment. Tomorrow I will go back there. I will search the old town again. Somewhere, there must be a clue to help me put the brakes on this runaway car.

Boy

Something wakes me, I don't know what. I open my eyes but keep very still. It takes me a second to remember that I'm not at home, that I'm inside an old train carriage.

Pale grey light glows through the window, but I sense it's no longer dusk. I have been asleep for longer. It must be dawn. I am about to brush the hair from my eyes, when I hear a noise coming from the opposite side of the compartment. An icy wave rushes over me. I keep absolutely still. Perhaps it's an animal sheltering from the rain, only it's not raining any more.

I swivel my eyes to the left, but whatever made the noise is beyond my field of vision. Perhaps I have blended into the shadows in my gloomy corner. If I stay still, then I might go unnoticed.

With every second that passes, the shapes in the compartment become a little sharper as more daylight

111

filters in. The silence is broken by a low coughing noise and I jump. The thing in the room is a person, and they must have just seen me move. There is silence again. Slowly, I turn my head. On the opposite side of the compartment, sitting wrapped in a sheet is a boy. He is staring at me.

I feel the thumping of my heart beneath my T-shirt. I stare back, waiting to see what he will do. He looks about my age. He doesn't turn away.

"Where's the other one?" he asks. When I don't answer, he repeats, "Where's the other one, the boy?"

I hesitate, trying to work out what's going on, but the boy keeps on staring.

"He's gone," I reply.

"Was he your brother?" the boy asks.

"Yes," I answer, wondering how he knows any of this stuff.

"You can't stay here," says the boy. "This is my place. You'll have to find somewhere else. Don't tell anyone about it. I'll know it was you." In the half light, he shrugs the sheet from his shoulders and throws it onto the heap next to him, then walks towards the hole in the floor. Before I can say anything else, in one fluid movement he slips down through it and out of the compartment.

"Wait!" I shout.

For a second, a head reappears in the hole. "Shh!" the boy says angrily. "I told you I don't want anyone to find this place," he hisses, then he disappears again.

I jump up and my head spins. I put my hand against the wall to steady myself, then I follow the boy. Lowering myself back through the hole is much harder than coming up, and I scrape my arms against the metal edges as I squeeze through.

I crawl out from beneath the train and run over to the tracks. The boy is far ahead, moving quickly towards the platforms. In the morning light I can see that he is wearing orange trousers. My head feels fuzzy from hunger. I can't work out where I've seen him before. Then it comes back to me.

"Stop!" I shout, ignoring his warning. "Come back!" He doesn't stop, or even turn around.

He was the boy standing under the tree in the rain, in a blue poncho. He was the one pushing a trolley, wearing Amit's T-shirt. That means he must have been with the boys who found us behind the luggage trunks that night, the ones who stole Amit's rucksack. They were the reason we had to hide. They made Amit cry. Maybe if I'd slept properly that first night, I wouldn't have been so tired the next day and made such a stupid mistake. Amit might still be here with me now if I'd held his hand in the crowd.

113

I feel my anger bubbling inside. I want to confront the boy straight away, but I know I won't be able to catch him. I keep walking anyway, until I reach the end of the platform. I sit, my legs dangling over the edge. My arms sting and I lift one up to see that the skin on the inside is red from where it scraped the edge of the hole, but not cut. As I look down, I notice that my jeans are filthy with black sooty mud. So are my hands and T-shirt.

As my anger fades, I almost want it to come back. The feeling which takes its place is both heavy and empty at the same time. This is the second day of my life which has started without my dad or my brother.

I push myself up and head towards the station toilet to wash my hands and see if I can clean off any of the dirt. I wish there was a mirror I could look in. I wish I could brush my hair and change my clothes. I wish I could go home.

It's still early so the toilets are empty. There is only a cold tap, and it's stiff. I manage to turn it enough for a trickle of water to dribble down and begin to rub my hands together. I wash my face and start to dab at the sooty marks on my jeans.

A woman walks in behind me. She tuts, and I turn round. She looks at me as if I am the source of the bad smell in the bathroom. She makes a shooing motion which herds me in the direction of the door. She looks at the sooty sink and tuts again. I stare at the woman as I walk back out into the ticket hall, but I can't think of anything to say. I would prefer to stay dirty than have her look at me that way.

Search

With a feeling of urgency which borders on panic, I walk to our apartment in the old town. Almost twenty-four hours have passed since I was there last. What if Dad or Amit have been waiting outside and decide that I'm not going to come? As I turn the last corner, a familiar flicker of hope begins to glow. I look up towards our apartment block, and an empty street. The windows are all shut. I don't know what I expected to see, what kind of sign.

I feel so weak; I can't make it back to the station again. I wander slowly down the narrow old streets towards the food stalls. The smell of cooking is overwhelming. My stomach twists painfully. Even though I have no money, I stop by the man making flatbreads. I watch him turn one and add it to a pile at the side. He looks up and waves me away. When I don't move, he picks up a flatbread which has torn and burnt a little.

As I turn to leave, he passes it to me. He doesn't smile or look at me. It feels like a gift for leaving, for moving on.

I sit on a step at the side of the street and tear small pieces from the flatbread. My mouth is dry, and I have to chew slowly. Straight away my body begins to feel better.

I walk a little further and see a polystyrene tray, left at the side of the road. There is fluffy white rice covered in some kind of sauce. It looks almost untouched. I imagine eating mouthful after mouthful, until the growling emptiness in my stomach goes away. I've seen street rats eat food from the floor and thought how disgusting they are, that no one could ever be so desperate. Around me people pass, chatting, carrying things, casting glances at me. Grey clouds are gathering overhead. It will rain soon. I walk away from the temptation of the meal, back towards the shelter of the station.

A group of boys approaches me from the opposite direction. I cross the street and walk as close to the buildings as I can without bumping into the walls. They shout over.

"Where's your boyfriend? Why has he let you come out on your own? Or doesn't he know?" They start to laugh.

One of the boys peels away from the others and crosses the road to my side of the street. He grabs my arm.

"Such a beautiful face," he says. "Why are you on your own?" I wrench my arm free and begin to run. "Make sure you go straight home," he shouts, sounding cross. "Next time I might not let you go."

I hear the other boys shouting behind me too, but their voices aren't getting any closer. As I turn the next corner, the enormous white roof of the station is in sight. I'm glad to see it, then shocked when I realize that a train station is taking the place of my real home.

Unlike my real home, there's no one here to welcome me. I pass what's left of the day in corners, around edges, searching, looking until my eyes ache.

When I can't search any more, I think about Mila, about the smile she would give me when I walked into the kitchen, even though I often didn't smile back. I let myself think about Dad. Somewhere inside I know that something bad has happened. When I begin to wonder what that might be, I shake my head to try and break the train of thought.

I lean against the wall as I daydream. The station street rats are beginning to pay me attention. They are all boys. All younger than me. Perhaps they've realized that I'm not travelling anywhere, or maybe it's because my clothes are a mess. They watch. They don't come near me though. I guess they're still not sure what I am. I'm not sure either.

I begin to watch them back. They walk over to passengers and point at their luggage. The passengers shoo them away or nod their heads. Carrying someone's luggage is better than eating food from the floor. If you carry someone's luggage then you get money to buy food instead.

As evening approaches, the station buzzes with people. A lady walks in pulling a suitcase in one hand. A large bag is slung over her other shoulder. I walk towards her.

"Excuse me," I say quietly, "would you like some help with your bags?"

She turns to look at me, confused. I don't look like the street rats. She pushes the handle of the suitcase towards me, but before I can take it from her, I feel a sharp pain at the back of my head. Someone is yanking my hair so hard that my head tips back in the air. While I can't move, a boy pushes in front of me. "Sorry," he says to the lady. "It's my sister's first time. She doesn't know what to do. I will take your bags."

"Platform four," says the lady. She doesn't seem to notice that someone is hurting me. My head jerks forwards as my hair is released and I see a young boy run after the older one.

As darkness settles outside the station, inside the lights seem brighter. I think about orange-trouser boy and the carriage. Anger swells inside me again. He took our things. He has a whole carriage to himself. I wonder if he was watching when I tried to carry bags earlier. Maybe he sent those boys over to pull my hair. I'm not going back to his carriage. I'll find somewhere better to sleep.

A girl walks past me dragging a piece of cardboard behind her. She can't be more than five years old. A boy trails after her with an armful of newspaper. I've seen street rats sleeping on sheets of cardboard. I follow them out of the ticket hall towards the tunnel which goes from the station, under the main road and comes out on the far side of the street. Street rats are gathered along both walls, laying out things to sleep on. Halfway along I see a small gap. I head there and sit down near a group of three boys, younger than me.

"Get lost," says the one nearest to me. "We're here. Find somewhere else."

I walk back towards the entrance. The walls are almost full on both sides. I find another small space and sit down, then curl up on the floor. It's cold and covered in a layer of grit, but if it looks like I'm asleep already, then maybe no one will ask me to move.

I wake to the sound of children chatting quietly, then later, to someone snoring softly. Soon after, is the noise of clanging metal and raised voices. I sit up and desperately try to remember where I am. The tunnel

121

is pitch black apart from two moving points of light at the far end. Torches. There is a thudding noise and a child cries out. I hear the soft patter of bare feet as street rats run past me to the entrance.

A man's voice shouts, "Get the other one—the girl." I know it's a different girl. He can't see me, but his voice is moving quickly in my direction.

I turn to follow the running rats. Up ahead, a dark shape fills the exit. Another man is waiting, lunging at the street rats, trying to grab one as they pass. There's only a trickle of them now. I've left it too late. He crouches down lower, his hands outstretched.

Behind me the shouts are getting closer. I run straight towards the guard as fast as I can and then at the very last second dart to the right. He reaches out and grasps my wrist, then he snatches at my hair. I writhe and pull away. Unbalanced, he falls to one knee. He is trying to drag me towards him, to get a firmer grip. I know that if he gets his arm round my waist, I won't be able to break free. I dip my head and clamp my teeth on to his hairy arm. I bite down as hard as I can. The man shouts out and pulls his arm back, giving me a few seconds to sprint out of the tunnel and onto the street.

From the tunnel come echoey cries, then a scream closer behind. The guard has caught another child, and he's really angry now.

I emerge on the opposite side of the main road to the station. Rows of bicycle rickshaws are lined up here, the legs of the sleeping drivers sprawling over the sides of the seats. The children from the tunnel have trickled like water down the streets and alleyways. Two men drinking tea near one of the streetlamps call over to me. I keep my head low and walk as if I know where I'm going, down one of the wider roads.

A little way along is a footbridge. As I get closer, I see there are lots of people sleeping underneath. They are a tangle of legs and cardboard and plastic sheets. Some street rats are curled up along the edge, and a mother is nursing a baby.

I sit quietly on the curb near them. My wrist is throbbing. The man who tried to catch me was wearing a uniform. He looked like a station guard. I remember feeling safe when I saw the guards before. I guess it's different now I don't have any money or place to go. I wonder what has happened to the children they caught. I feel sick as I remember the salty taste of the man's wrist.

I look over at the mother and baby and think of Mila. I wonder what she sleeps on in the slums. Whether she has a proper bed. I wonder why I've never thought about it before. Wrapping my arms round my knees, I wait for dawn. Only the thought that I might find Amit or Dad tomorrow gives me strength.

Boy

I watch the sun rise behind the apartment. After an hour, the security guard wakes up. He spots me waiting opposite the gate and waves at me to go away.

Storm clouds are gathering overhead as I stop at the breakfast stall. The man isn't happy to see me. I wait quietly. After he's served two customers, he flips a small pile of burnt scrapings onto a piece of paper and throws it towards me. I feel ashamed. I am a nuisance. A girl who is sneaking around without permission. I'm not Lola to anyone.

I search up and down alleyways, then—when my legs are almost too weak to carry on—I head back to the station.

Standing near the rickshaws are four girls in bright dresses. It must be the weekend. My heart skips a beat. What if they are from my school? Although it's a long way from their part of town, it's the holidays, and this is one of the biggest train stations in the city.

I walk past as quickly as I can, and glance over. One of the girls sees me looking.

"Don't stare," she says, "you might make my dress dirty." Her friends giggle. She turns back to talk to them. They're not from my school. Three steps later, they will have completely forgotten that I exist.

I pick my way through the rickshaws and crowds to find a corner in the ticket hall where I can watch people come and go. Seeing those girls makes me think about Bella. I wonder what she thinks has happened to me. If I could find my way to her house, perhaps her family would let me stay for a while. But then I would be on the other side of the city. I can't bear to be so far from where I lost Amit, and from our apartment, where I might find Dad.

I think again about telling Bella what's happened to me when it's all over. She will be amazed by my story. About how I couldn't wash my hair and I had to wear the same clothes all the time. She'll want to know how much I could fit in my rucksack, and how I coped without television for more than a week.

Until Dad comes back, though, I'm not sure either Bella or I would be able to make any of this seem funny. I look down at my fingernails. The varnish has mostly peeled off. One bottle of nail varnish might cost the same as food for a whole week, if you live at the station.

A train from some far-off city thuds and creaks its way slowly towards a platform. It has lots of carriages, and hundreds of passengers. I know, because the same train arrived yesterday. Street rats appear like smoke, drifting through the ticket hall towards passengers with bags and cases. Like smoke, the passengers wave them away or ignore them. Sometimes they point to bags or taxis, and rats scurry to help, their thin arms pulling fat cases. No one says thank you, not that I see anyway. I need money, but I don't have the strength to lift anything.

I rest my head against the wall as a squeal of pain echoes across the shiny floor. It's high-pitched, like the voice of a small child. Through the crowd I see the top half of a guard, his arm above his head, as if ready to strike.

I scramble to my feet and run towards the sound. A rat, younger than Amit, cowers on the floor next to the guard as a girl tugs at his hand, trying to drag him clear. The boy lets out a terrified whimper as the guard brings his baton down again, striking the boy's shoulder with a thump.

I feel my legs move and in a few steps I reach the boy and grab his free hand, pulling him from beneath the guard. The baton strikes me instead. The force knocks me to the ground and I feel a shock of pain in the middle of my back. I look up to see the guard raising his baton again, but I am too fast. I roll to the side, then get to my feet and run towards the platforms. There is no sound of footsteps behind me, but I can't risk going back to the ticket hall.

I choose the most crowded platform and keep going, my back throbbing. The sky has begun to darken, and I know it's not rain clouds overhead. Night is coming again. I move silently past the last of the passengers, towards the sidings. As I jump down onto the gravel, pain explodes again in the middle of my back. I wait for it to pass, then walk towards the old train carriages, past the rusting overgrown compartments, until I come to the last one.

I get down on my hands and knees and crawl underneath, then lie still on the sooty gravel, while my eyes adjust to the darkness.

After a few minutes I can make out the faint greyish glow, in the shape of a circle. I crawl towards it and then turn round carefully to a sitting position. I keep still for a few more seconds, listening for sounds from inside the carriage. I hear only car horns honking in the distance.

I poke my head through the hole and look around the space. The pile of sheets is still in the corner, otherwise it's empty. I haul the rest of my body up through the hole and sit down in the same corner as before, trying to find a comfortable way of leaning against the carriage. I don't know how long I will have to wait. My back feels hot, and when the sore part touches the wall I breathe in sharply.

I wonder where the little boy and girl will sleep tonight. Some of the kids at my school used to laugh about using rats for target practice. *Moving targets are better.* So I don't know why I was surprised that none of the passengers told the guard to stop beating a rat, even if the rat was only four or five.

I must be dozing when I hear a gentle swishing sound. The sound of a body sliding up through the hole. I freeze. Moonlight slices through the window onto the smooth cheekbones of a boy. It's the same boy, and he is staring at me angrily.

"I told you not to come back," he says.

I can feel my heart thumping near the top of my chest. "Where's my rucksack?" I answer.

"This is my carriage," he says. "I don't share it with anyone."

My mouth is dry. "Where's my rucksack?" I ask again. I pause. "I'm not leaving without it."

"I don't have your stupid rucksack. Get. Out. Now," he says, walking towards me. I push myself against the side of the carriage but don't move my eyes away from his. I dig the nails of one hand into the palm of the other. It helps me to feel calmer.

"I'm not leaving," I whisper.

He paces in front of me, then raises his hand towards me quickly. I lift my arm to protect my face, but he slams his palm onto the side of the carriage instead. "I don't have your rucksack. You can't stay here, this is my place. Only mine."

"I'm not leaving. There's nowhere else to go," I reply. The voice doesn't feel like mine.

"There are plenty of places, if you look."

"Fine. Then show me where, and I'll go."

It's crazy to speak to him like this. But I have absolutely nothing to lose now. He stops pacing and stares at me again. Then he walks over to the pile of sheets in the opposite corner and sits down, still glaring at me.

He reaches for a package which wasn't there before. He peels back the paper and takes out some kind of sandwich. He starts to eat. My stomach twists painfully. For a few minutes he just bites and chews. When he's finished, he screws up the piece of paper and wipes his hands on his T-shirt. I look at it more closely and realize that it belongs to Amit. Tears spring up and I blink them away.

"You stole my brother's rucksack, and now he is on his own without anything." A sob rises up in my chest and I can't stop it.

He looks up, surprised that I'm crying. "You shouldn't

have been so stupid as to sleep out in the open like that with a big rucksack full of stuff."

"So you did take it?"

He doesn't say anything for a few seconds. "First you said it was your rucksack, now you say it was your brother's. Maybe you stole it from someone too?"

"He's only eight," I say. "You should feel ashamed of yourself."

"It's not about age. It's about common sense. There are plenty of kids here who are four. Even they would have had the common sense to hide a rucksack, if they had one."

"Four?" I say. He stares at me. I stop digging my nails into my palm.

He yawns. "I want to go to sleep," he says. "You're stopping me."

"If you let me stay then I will get some food for both of us tomorrow."

As soon as the words have left my mouth I regret saying them. He snorts, and I realize that he's laughing. "You won't get food," he says. "I've been watching you. Tomorrow you'll get nothing. Lots of it." He laughs again at his joke. "You can sleep here tonight, but only because I can't be bothered to make you leave. Tomorrow I want you gone. And make sure no one sees you leave in the morning. No one. Understand?"

"Yes," I say meekly. "My name is Lola." He doesn't reply.

I curl up on the floor. It's hard and I'm cold, but I know that I will sleep tonight. I think of Amit, and hope that he is somewhere safe. I wish with every fibre of my body that he was lying on the other side of the compartment wearing that grey T-shirt, instead of the boy who stole it from him.

Trip

When I wake, rain is drumming on the roof of the train compartment. I sit up, but before I even look over to the other side of the room, I know that orange-trouser boy will be gone. My head spins and my stomach hurts. I stand up and notice that my jeans are beginning to feel loose round my waist. I look again at the pile of sheets in the corner. Perhaps Amit's rucksack is under there. I don't look. I don't want to see anything of his right now. Not while he is somewhere else.

I slide down through the hole, being careful to lift my arms higher so that they don't scrape on the sides. I crawl out from under the carriage and into the rain. I look around but can't see anyone nearby, so I walk over to the adjacent tracks, away from the carriage, and follow them towards the platforms. I don't care about getting wet. Perhaps it will clean off some of the dirt.

As I walk along the platform, I realize how different I look to the passengers waiting for their trains. I am dirty and my hair is unbrushed, but I sense there is something else too. I carry everything with me now, inside. I cannot leave any part of me lying safely elsewhere. There is nowhere else. Maybe that makes me walk in a different way, look at other people in a different way. Whatever it is, I feel like it is the first part of becoming a street rat. Or maybe it's the last part.

At the apartment, there is no one. The man at the breakfast stall tells me to go away. I must get something to give to the boy in the carriage. Anything. I look around in desperation and see a branch of bananas suspended outside a shop selling drinks. There is no shopkeeper outside. As I walk past, I tug at one of the fruits. It comes away but my tug makes the canopy sway. A man comes out but I keep walking without turning round. No one points at me or shouts that I stole from him. No one saw.

As I walk, a rickshaw rings its bell and two boys in the back make kissing noises as it passes.

I lean against the wall on the far side of the ticket hall. I need to eat the banana, but I need somewhere to sleep tonight too.

After a little while, a train pulls in and spills out hundreds of passengers. A large group of women enter the ticket hall from the platform, talking and laughing.

They have lots of bags and suitcases. I push myself away from the wall and walk quickly towards them, aiming for the closest woman. Before I get there a boy runs in front of me and taps her on the shoulder. "You need help with your bags?" He already has a hand on her suitcase. I look around for someone else to help, but now they all have a street rat.

I go back to the wall. For the first time since I left our apartment, I want it to get dark sooner. There is nothing fun to fill the rest of my day, nothing to look forward to. I could sit here until the evening without moving, and perhaps no one would even notice.

As I watch people come and go, I become aware of something beside me. I turn, with a start, to see a little boy standing next to me. I didn't hear him arrive. He looks up at me and smiles.

"Thank you for saving me yesterday."

I find myself smiling back. "That's OK. I didn't exactly save you."

"You did," comes a voice from my other side. I turn to see the girl standing to my right. "That guard doesn't stop. He likes beating us." She moves round to sit on the same side as the boy. "What's your name?" she asks.

"Lola," I answer.

"That's a pretty name," she says. "I'm Pia and this is Mo."

135

The boy looks maybe four or five. He shuffles closer and puts his hand inside mine. His hand is warm and dry, and small.

"Why was the guard beating you?" I ask Mo.

"Got in the way," he says.

"Where are your mum and dad?"

The girl's smile fades and she twists her mouth to one side. "They're back home," she says.

"Shall we go and find them?" I say.

The girl looks at me, confused. "They're not here," she says. "They're in our village."

Now I'm confused. "So how did you get to the station?" I ask.

"We came on a train," the boy says, looking at me as if I'm quite silly.

"Mum and Dad didn't come with us," adds the girl.

I stare at them both, trying to work out what happened.

"It's because we didn't have enough to eat," says the girl. "We have older brothers and sisters too. They work, but there still wasn't enough food for everyone. Or jobs. I thought that maybe in the city Mo and I might get some work. Everyone is looking for work here too though. We can't go back home with nothing. We've been here a while now. Maybe three weeks, maybe six weeks. I'm not sure."

I nod. I put my other hand out for the girl to take.

"Can I play with your hair?" she asks.

"Sure. Can you do plaits?"

She nods. I sit down, leaving a gap between me and the wall for Pia to walk around. As she starts to gather some hair from one side of my head, Mo lays his head on my leg and closes his eyes.

"What do you do?" I ask. "When you're not making beautiful plaits."

Pia grins. "Mostly we go to find the banana man. He has a big truck and he parks it near here. He gives us bananas to sell. He lets us keep a little bit of money if we sell them all. Some days we don't eat though, if we don't sell enough, or sometimes he's not there."

After five minutes or so, Pia says, "I've finished."

Mo sits up to have a look.

"You have nice hair. It's very straight."

I run my hands down both sides of my head and feel two thick, even plaits snaking down towards my back. "Very good!" I say.

Pia smiles. "You look like a movie star."

"Do you sleep at the station too?" asks Mo.

"Yes. I haven't been here as long as you though."

"Do you have brothers and sisters?" he asks.

"I have a little brother called Amit," I say. "But I lost him in a crowd, and now I don't know how to find him.

He really could be a movie star one day. He's good at singing and dancing."

"We can help you find him," says Mo. His eyes are shining with excitement.

"Then he can sing and dance for us!" says Pia.

"I think he'd love that," I say.

Dusk begins to fall with a soft pattering of rain, which quickly becomes a loud thrumming sound on the station roof.

Pia looks anxiously round the ticket hall. Some rats are already heading towards the exit to find somewhere to sleep for the night.

"We need to go," she says to Mo. "We have a special secret place to sleep. You're too big, but maybe tomorrow we can help you find somewhere else good," she says, looking at me.

"Thank you," I say.

They both nod and walk towards the exit.

I don't get up straight away. Instead I sit for a while and watch the steady trickle of rats on their way to find a place to lie down, without dinner, or a cuddle, or someone saying goodnight.

I liked it when Pia gave me plaits. She made fun as we rested at the side of the ticket hall. Like a seed growing, she found some light, however faint. I wonder what she could do, what she could be, if she didn't have to sell bananas for hours every day; if she had more than the roads and the station as her playground. The roads and station might be my future now, too.

I get to my feet and head in the opposite direction, towards the sidings, slipping off the platform end onto the gravel.

Haircut

When I reach the final carriage I am soaked. I pull myself into the empty compartment and take the banana from my pocket, placing it on top of my knees.

When orange-trouser boy emerges through the hole, he glances at me then moves silently to his corner and thumps down on the floor. He seems to be in a bad mood. "What are you doing here again?" he says, glaring at me.

"I brought food," I say, "you said I could stay if I brought food." He said he didn't believe I could get food, which is different, but I don't care. I place the banana on the floor in front of him.

"Is that it?" he says.

I nod.

He peels away the skin and eats the banana in three bites. He doesn't offer me any. When he's finished, he places the skin on the floor next to him.

I look at the empty fruit and feel hot tears pool in my eyes. One of them spills down my cheek. I don't have the energy to brush it away. The boy ignores me and takes a small packet out from under his T-shirt. I hear a tinkle of coins as he empties its contents onto the floor and starts sliding coins into two piles. His head snaps up.

"What are you looking at?" he asks.

"Nothing," I say, and turn to look up at the compartment window. I think about how Dad would always try to make me laugh when I was sad. He would pull silly faces or tease me.

When Mum died, I can remember Dad being sad more clearly than I remember feeling sad myself. I would give anything to see his face right now. To hear his voice. I wonder whether Amit is feeling as sad as me. Perhaps he has nothing to eat either. He used to eat non-stop when we were at home. He'd always get hungry before I did. A terrible thought flashes into my head. What if he starves before I find him?

There is a noise. I jump, and realize that the boy is talking. I turn my head and see that he is staring at me.

"You should cut your hair," he repeats.

I can't work out if my hunger is making me confused. Why does he care what my hair looks like? I don't answer.

"Did you hear me? You need to cut your hair."

142

I hold his gaze and say quietly, "I haven't got any money. I haven't eaten for about a week. Why would I go for a haircut?" As I speak, his idea seems even more ridiculous than it did at first.

He laughs. "You really don't know anything, do you?"

"I probably know a lot more about having a haircut than you do," I say, looking at his thick, sticking-up hair.

"Fine, Miss Know-nothing-useful. Have it your way," he says crossly. "You gave me some food for your rent for last night. What about tonight?"

"I'll have to find something tomorrow," I say.

I'm not sure I can survive another day without some food for myself, and I need to get something for the boy too.

I don't understand why he's interested in my hair, but I can't afford to annoy the orange-trouser boy either. After a minute or so I say, "OK, so why do I need a haircut?"

He raises his eyebrows and smiles in a way which says he has won. "I know a place where they will cut all your hair off and give you money for it."

"Money, just for my hair? They'd pay me?" He's even weirder than I thought.

"They might pay a lot for yours. It's really long."

"I've been to the hairdresser loads of times, and I've never ever seen the hairdresser give anyone money for their hair."

"Different kind of shop," the boy says simply. "I bet you only ever have a tiny bit cut off. In the places I'm talking about, they take all your hair. The longer the better. They turn your hair into wigs or hair extensions and sell them to rich people."

I hold a lock of my hair in my hand and imagine it on someone else's head. I can't remember ever having short hair. Me and my friends all have long hair. I think about Pia carefully stroking it, weaving it into plaits.

"Anyway, it's better for you to have short hair."

"How can it be better to have hair like a boy?" As soon as I say the words, I realize what he means. If I have short hair, people might actually believe I am a boy. Maybe I won't get stared at so much. No one would think it was OK to stroke my hair any more. Perhaps the rats won't think they can just push me around.

"It's just better," he snaps. He's glaring angrily at the floor again.

I don't know what I said to annoy him.

After a few minutes of silence, he says, "Tomorrow I will take you to the hair shop."

"OK," I say quietly. Then I add, "Thank you."

"Don't thank me," he says. He tugs at one of the sheets next to him and straightens it out on the floor before lying down.

I lie down too, curled up in the opposite corner. My cheek rests on a thick lock of hair. I notice it draped over my neck in a way that I haven't before. I can hear the boy moving restlessly around. Something heavy lands on my feet and I sit up with a yelp.

"It's just a sheet," says the boy. "My name is Rafi." Before I have a chance to reply, he lies down again with his back to me.

I sleep fitfully. Hunger stops me from falling deeply asleep. When I finally open my eyes, it's past dawn. I sit up and see that Rafi is already awake, leaning against the wall of the compartment, staring at the ceiling.

"Good afternoon," he says. I feel the corners of my mouth twitch up in a smile, before a wave of sadness wipes it away as I remember Dad saying the same thing whenever I was late for breakfast.

"Let's go," says Rafi. "Haircut."

He slides through the hole and I scramble after him. Rafi's feet press silently on the platform floor. He walks lightly and carefully, like a cat. He nods to a group of kids in the ticket hall but doesn't slow down.

We walk through the tunnel where I was nearly caught by the guard and emerge on the opposite side of the big road. I'm a few paces behind, struggling to keep up. After maybe five minutes, he darts down a narrow street. The rough cement walls are dotted with wonky metal doors. Some plain, others with curling designs in faded paint. Men lean against the wall, chatting. They stare at Rafi and me.

He stops outside a pale-blue door and turns to face me.

"Wait here," he says, raising his hand a bit like a traffic policeman.

I lean against the wall and stare at my feet, avoiding the stares of the chatting men.

Rafi pokes his head through the door and waves me in. I walk through a small room with a few chairs, to another room, where a man stands next to a stool. I'm glad Rafi is with me.

"Sit down," the man says, without smiling.

As soon as I am seated, a woman enters. She is small and wears a bright-pink shawl. She doesn't smile either. She unpicks my plaits, then from within the folds of her shawl she produces a pair of silver scissors. She pulls a lock of my hair out straight and snips as close to my head as possible. She then lays the lock on a small table, with far more care than she cut it.

The woman gathers lock after lock. The hair on the table grows into a pile, and my head begins to feel light and strange. When she's finished snipping, there is no mirror to look in. I reach up to touch my hair. It feels smooth in places and spiky in others.

The man returns and inspects the hair on the table. He takes some notes from his pocket and gives them to Rafi then walks over to gather up my hair. He doesn't turn round or say anything to me. I get up from the stool and follow Rafi, who is already halfway through the door, stuffing the notes under his T-shirt.

It takes a few fast steps for me to catch up with him. I tap him on the shoulder.

"Can I have the money please?" I say.

"Shut up," he snaps back, walking more quickly. I feel heads turning as we walk. There is no hair for me to hide behind.

Everyone here knows my awful truth, that I went in with beautiful long hair, and have come out with it clipped short and rough like a boy.

"Hey," I say more loudly.

This time Rafi doesn't answer or turn round, but just keeps on walking. He turns left at the end of the street and keeps going. Ten metres or so on, he darts down an alleyway. I run after him. I turn the corner and see he has stopped a short way down. I am out of breath and my head is spinning.

"You stole my money!" I shout, just as my legs buckle beneath me and I sit down heavily at the side of the alleyway.

Rafi comes over and shoves something roughly onto

my leg. I look down and see a small bundle of notes. He is glaring at the top of my head, his lips thin.

"I didn't steal your money. There's half. Everyone in that alleyway would have happily taken the money straight from your hands if ▮ given it to you there and then. It didn't help that you kept shouting about it too."

"I'm sorry," I say, closing my hand round the notes. I barely have the energy to speak.

"You should get something to eat," he says, then he steps over my legs and disappears round the corner of the alleyway.

Nothing I learnt at school feels any use to me now. No one teaches you what to do when everything you care about has been taken away. Every time I think I have nothing more to lose, another little piece of Lola falls away, or is snipped off and laid out in a neat pile on a table beside me.

I know I can't change what has already happened, but perhaps I can slow the speeding car down, little by little. I need to start thinking more like Rafi. Rafi knows how to use what little he's got. There's something, someone, who I wanted to keep safely in my old life, ready for when I return to it. But I need her now. Bella.

Bella

I pass our apartment without stopping. On the pavement outside are the remains of a marigold necklace, flattened into a darker shade of orange by last night's rain. The man at the breakfast stand doesn't recognize me. I take a note from my bundle and buy one flatbread. I eat it slowly, then I buy another one and start walking. I have three notes left.

As my stomach fills, a different emptiness creeps in. The longer I am apart from Dad and Amit, the more I feel as if the distance between us is growing.

I know which direction to go in, but not the best route. The narrow streets with beautiful, crumbling stone walls join up with a wide road, a metal barrier running through the middle. Either side is a lane of cars and trucks, then large rickshaws, then small rickshaws and bicycles. Vehicles criss-cross in front of each other as horns honk and bells tinkle.

I walk at the side of the road, car fumes wafting around me. I step around pots and pans, brooms and umbrellas—the contents of the roadside shops that have spilled out from under their makeshift plastic roofs.

Now that I am a scruffy boy, no one pays me much attention. As I walk, I see street rats tapping on car windows to ask if they need a wipe. I see them lying at the side of the road asleep. Under bridges are whole families shrouded in plastic and newspaper. Everywhere I look I see people gathered like the rubbish carried by rainwater, also with nowhere to go, until someone sweeps them up and takes them away.

I run through what I want to say to Bella. I get as far as Dad going missing, but I can't think of how to explain the rest. That I've been staying in a hotel. That I lost Amit when we were shopping. That I cut my hair off because we had no proper shower and it just looked such a mess. I'm not sure what sounds normal any more, but I know the truth will sound like fiction.

Should it matter at all what my story sounds like? It's not the same as the things we share at break times and lunchtimes. It's nothing funny or silly. I'm in real trouble. Friends help each other when they're in trouble. I feel a glow of hope. I begin to wish I'd told Bella everything sooner. The last few weeks might have been so different.

After a couple of hours, the road rises up and away from the shops below; a flyover which loops in a semi-circle then descends into the rich part of town. I hug the side of the road as cars travel quickly here. At the bottom of the loop I enter a grid of streets with large square houses, each with a gate and a garden front and back.

There is a fluttery feeling in my stomach. Maybe Bella will be out. It's still the school holidays, I think, and she goes away a lot.

My feet are hot and I can feel the side of my right little toe beginning to rub on my trainers. At least it's not raining.

I turn onto a street which feels familiar, but it's not Bella's. At the end, I turn another corner. I spot Bella's house a little further down, wider and taller than the other buildings. There is a vehicle parked in the drive-way. My heart starts to beat more quickly.

As I walk up to the gate, a man in a brown uniform appears. He waves his hands as if to shoo me away.

"Is Bella at home?" I ask. The security guard looks confused. "Could you please tell her that her friend Lola is outside?"

The guard stares at me. He wants to send me away, but I can see that a little part of him is worried he might get into trouble. He goes into a hut and I hear him talking. Seconds later, there is movement by one of the windows. I look up but can't see anybody. The gate doesn't open, nor does the front door.

"Hey!" I shout to the guard.

He appears at the entrance to his hut.

"Nobody has heard of a Lola. You've got the wrong house," he says, and disappears back inside. I cross the road so that I can see Bella's house more clearly. One of the blinds moves. Somebody is watching me.

"Bella! It's me! It's Lola!" I shout. The shadow behind the blind seems to grow bigger; the blind clatters against the window but no figure appears. "Bella, I need to talk to you. Amit is missing," I shout.

The guard comes out of his hut and walks towards the gate. He opens the smaller gate at the side, the one for people not cars. I feel my legs move and realize I am running towards the guard, towards the open gate. I dodge round him and into the courtyard. I bound up the three steps and bang on the front door.

"Bella! Dad is missing and now Amit is missing too." I feel a large hand grip my arm and pull me away from the door and down the steps. I stumble to stay upright. The guard pushes me through the open gate and out onto the street, where I fall on one knee.

"Go! Leave," he says, "unless you want me to beat you too." I twist round and see that he is holding a rubber baton, like the type the station guards and the police use. I glance up at the silent faceless house and get to my feet, then I start walking slowly down the street, the way I came.

Why? Why did nobody open the door? Why?

If Bella saw me, she would have come straight away. Wouldn't she? It must have been her mother's shadow at the window. But why would her mother leave me standing on the street? Is it possible Bella's mother wouldn't let her see me?

These thoughts go round and round, like one of Amit's songs.

I need to think of a new way to stop the speeding car now. What do I have left?

As I turn the corner at the end of Bella's road, I feel a sharp pain on the back of my leg. I bend down to see what it is and something hits me hard on the cheek. A stone skitters into the road. I stand up and start to run. More stones skitter onto the road behind. People don't want rats in this part of town. Someone is using me for target practice.

I keep running, even though I barely have the energy to walk. I make myself remember that when the kids at school laughed about using rats for target practice, I laughed too. Not because I thought it was funny, but because I wasn't brave enough to say it wasn't. I might as well have been the one throwing stones.

Famous

As the white roof of the station comes into view, a large raindrop lands on my arm. I hear the patter as more hit the pavement. There are raised voices and people run past me as everyone rushes to escape the rain. A stream of passengers enters the ticket hall from the other side. A train has just arrived. I weave my way towards them and spot a lady and her elderly mother. I go up to the younger woman and point to her suitcase. I feel myself being pushed to one side and turn to see a boy who is younger than me staring back. Before he can take the suitcase instead, someone else pulls him away. Standing next to me, is Rafi.

"Quick," he nods towards the woman, "or she'll be gone."

I pick up two large bags and head to the exit. I wave at a taxi and then stagger out through the puddles. After three journeys, the bags are all loaded in the boot. As she gets in the car the woman presses a small coin into my hand. I say thank you, blinking the rainwater from my eyes, but she doesn't look up.

I stand in the rain for a few more seconds. I've never felt it touch my head straight from the sky; not without thick hair to catch it first. I spot Rafi nearby with a couple who have two large suitcases. After a few seconds he places a small bag on his head, then with a suitcase handle in each hand he looks over at me and spins round like a ballerina, then melts into the crowd by the exit.

I don't wait to see if he comes back. I don't look for any more passengers with bags to carry. I'm so tired I can barely stand. Slowly, I make my way to the end of the platform, limping slightly from where my trainer rubs against my toe. I have to go and sleep.

I open my eyes and see Rafi hauling himself up into the dark carriage. I close them again and listen as he sits down quietly. I hear the soft clink of coins being counted out. In the silence which follows, I sense that he is looking at me. Then I think he lies down, and everything is quiet in the carriage, except for the rhythm of the rain falling on the roof.

I wake first. Rafi is still lying asleep on his side, facing me. He looks younger when he's sleeping. His eyelashes are long for a boy. About the same length as mine. He has a scar on the left side of his chin. His eyes flick open. "What are you staring at?" he says.

When I don't answer, he sits up and runs his fingers through his stack of hair. I sense he is about to leave. I don't want to be on my own again today. I am becoming a watcher. Just a pair of eyes.

"Thanks for taking me to the hair shop," I say.

Rafi stops fiddling with his hair and laughs. "Hair shop!" he says. "That's a good name for a shop."

I can't tell if he's laughing at me or he really just thought it was a funny name.

"And thanks for helping me with the suitcases as well."

He rolls his eyes. "You are so clueless. It was embarrassing to watch. The six-year-olds are better than you."

"Yeah, well I hadn't planned on being a street rat," I say.

"None of us planned to be street rats," he says.

"How long have you been here?" I ask.

"I don't know," he answers. "Maybe a year." He looks down at his feet.

I preferred it when Rafi was laughing at me. I want to keep the conversation going.

"I don't know how to find my brother," I say. "I've searched all over the streets where we used to live, and all over this place."

He bends one of his toes backwards and forwards. It looks like he's deep in thought. "You might as well stop looking. You'll never find him." He says it like there is no doubt. Like I'm stupid to even look.

"Well I'm never going to give up," I say. "He'll be looking for me too. We've probably walked down the same roads looking for each other. I just have to be patient."

"That's what I used to think," Rafi says quietly.

"What do you mean?" I say.

He's still looking at his feet. "I mean," he says, "that maybe you're not the only person looking for somebody they've lost."

"Oh," I say.

He slams a hand down on the floor, which makes me jump. Then he stands up and walks over to the hole in the floor.

"He was going to be famous," I say quickly, hoping to draw him back in.

Rafi stops and turns round. "What do you mean, famous?"

"Like a movie star. He had an audition lined up—a proper one."

"Really?" says Rafi. "That," he smiles, "is definitely news." He pauses for a second, like he's thinking something over. "What did you say he was wearing the day you lost each other?"

"Jeans and a red T-shirt," I say. "What does it matter? I thought you said there was no way of ever finding him?"

"Yeah," says Rafi. "I did. But there's no harm in me looking out for him. See you later, I've got to be somewhere," he says as he slides down to the gravel beneath.

"Where?" I say, and then when he doesn't answer, "See you later," to the space Rafi disappeared from seconds before.

My head is buzzing. I want to feel cross, but instead I feel guilty that I said something which upset him. I play Rafi's last words back in my head: *"See you later."* A tiny spark of happiness flickers somewhere inside. I know that I am going to see someone later. I roll my socks up over the red blisters on the sides of my toes and ankles and pull my trainers on.

Everything is sore and achy from my walk to Bella's house. I'd felt a spark of happiness on my way there, too. It occurs to me that Bella might also be upset with me. Upset because I hadn't told her about the audition, upset that I hadn't turned up on Saturday. Could that be why no one let me in? But if she'd seen me outside her house, Bella would have realized that something was very wrong. I can't help thinking it was her mother who didn't want me there. Friend of her daughter's or not, I look like a rat.

Hurt

The blank walls of the apartment block seem to be judging me, the windows noting my return, day after day. I run my hand over my short hair. I wonder if Dad would even recognize me now. I walk away, stepping on a necklace of marigold flowers, squashed flat; another necklace, slightly brighter and newer lying alongside it.

Back at the station I wait outside in the rain by the taxis and rickshaws. The only difference in appearance now between me and the other street rats, is that I have trainers.

After an hour or so, I help an old man carry his luggage into the station. I am soaked, but no one pushes me out of the way. I spent more on food than I earned today, but it feels reassuring to make a few coins. Even a few coins can keep you alive, and I still have one note left from my haircut.

I head towards the place where metal trunks are piled up and sit down in the quiet space behind. I take my shoes off and wring my socks out, glad that my short hair doesn't drip rainwater down my back. It dries quickly too.

As I slip my second trainer back on, I become aware of someone watching me. I turn my head and see Pia and Mo peering round one of the trunks.

"It is her," Pia says, without taking her eyes off me.

They sit down in front of me, their expressions serious.

"What happened?" Pia asks.

"To what?" I say.

"To your hair."

"I cut it short. It dries faster and it doesn't get all tangled."

Pia touches her hair with her hand. "But you look like a boy."

"I wanted to look like a boy," I say. Pia looks at me, a little crease of confusion between her eyebrows. "People don't pull my hair any more."

Pia nods. "I don't want to look like a boy," she says.

"We've been looking for you," says Mo, jiggling around excitedly. "We have something to tell you!"

"Yes!" says Pia, her eyes sparkling with excitement. "Good news!"

"What is it?" I ask, glancing from face to face.

Mo giggles with delight. "We've found your brother!"

"What?" I say, my expression frozen. A rush of excitement buzzes through my chest. I try to think clearly. They've never even met Amit—how could they know it is him? "What does he look like?" I ask quietly.

"A bit bigger than Pia," Mo says.

"He had messy hair," Pia adds. "He was singing. He was really good. People waited even though it was raining."

I stand up. My legs feel a little shaky. "Can you show me?"

Mo claps his hands in happiness then holds one out for me to take. "We'll show you!"

The rain has nearly stopped. We hurry past the jumble of taxis and rickshaws and across the main road. I'm worried we might not get there in time. What if he moves to a new spot, looking for more customers? Pia walks quickly ahead. Mo clings to my hand, taking small running steps to keep up.

"He looks like you," chatters Mo. "Especially now that you've cut your hair."

Pia walks along the main road towards the footbridge. Just before we reach it, she turns round and says, "There! Look, he's there!"

She points to a small figure, bending down to count something on the floor. My heart thuds in my chest.

As we get closer, the boy stands up and looks in our direction. He is younger than Amit, and thinner.

Pia and Mo are watching me. They see my expression change and realize he's not the right boy. I feel my energy drain away.

Mo looks up anxiously, "He's not your brother?"

I shake my head. I can't seem to think of anything to say.

Pia walks to join us. "I'm sorry we found the wrong boy."

I crouch down next to them. "Thank you," I manage to say, "thank you for looking." I put my hand in my pocket and pull out the coins I earned this morning. I give one to Pia and one to Mo. They curl their fingers tightly round them and smile at me. We head back to the station together.

"Where's the banana man today?" I ask as we walk.

"He wasn't there," says Pia. "Someone said the roads were too bad. Should we look for you at night-time?" she asks.

"I thought you had a special place to sleep?" I say.

"We do," says Pia. "Maybe we could help you find somewhere good?"

"I have a place to sleep tonight," I tell them. "I'm hoping that soon there might be space there for you too. Would you like that?"

Pia and Mo look at each other, eyes sparkling. They turn to me and nod.

"I'm hungry," says Mo. "Can we spend our coins?" he asks Pia.

Pia holds her hand out for Mo to take, waving to me with the other. "Thank you for the money!" she says. They head out of the station towards the food stalls.

As soon as they are gone, I remember how it felt when the boy they'd found looked up from counting his coins. I ached with longing to see Amit's face instead of his. I wonder whose face he longed to see.

I start looking for luggage to carry. My body feels heavy and tired, but I need money. As I scan the ticket hall, I notice street rats lying near the wall. No one has any energy by the afternoon. Unless they slept in a bed and had food to eat for breakfast and lunch.

It takes me a while, but I make back the money I gave Pia and Mo. When it's mostly just the sleeper trains left to fill, I head to the carriage.

I'm later than normal, but when I slide up into the compartment, I see that it's empty. There's no sign of Rafi. I wonder where he goes, how he makes his money. I hardly ever see him carrying luggage.

I wrap myself in the sheet which Rafi gave me. While I wait for him to come back, I listen to the soft tinkling of rickshaw bells on the main road. My thoughts drift to

Bella's house and why no one came to the door. Maybe it was one of the housekeepers standing behind the blind. But their car was in the drive. Bella and her mum never walk anywhere.

I wake with a start. A scrabbling sound moves rapidly across the roof above my head, followed by a high-pitched screech. Monkeys. I sit up slowly and rub my eyes. Daylight fills the compartment and I hear a different kind of screech, the screech of train brakes followed by doors slamming. The rest of the city has been up for a while.

The carriage is empty and Rafi's sheets are still piled in the corner. A coldness spreads down through my body.

I wrap my arms round my knees. I stay like that for a long time. I put my socks and trainers on. Just as I'm about to get up I hear a noise on the gravel outside. There is a scraping sound, followed by something dragging itself along the gravel towards the hole underneath the compartment. I freeze. It can't be Rafi. He doesn't make any sound.

My heart thuds in my chest. As silently as possible, I walk to the opposite side of the carriage and pick up a couple of sheets. I crouch down on the floor and throw them over my head, making sure my body is covered, leaving a tiny hole which I can see through.

Perhaps whoever is underneath the carriage won't be able to fit through the hole. Or if they can, I will have a chance to slip down through it before they realize what is going on.

I see a hand come up through the hole and rest on the side, then another. Then I see the shape of someone pulling themselves very slowly through the gap. I try hard to stop myself from making a noise, but a yelp of fear bursts out.

Once the figure is through the hole, it turns immediately to where I am hiding. I stop breathing. It staggers a little towards me, and I can't bear it any longer. I throw the sheets off and dart towards the hole. Before I get there I shoot a look at the shape in the middle of the compartment. I stop so suddenly that I stumble to the ground. The figure is a boy covered in blood. He staggers a little bit more and then collapses against the wall.

"Oh my god, Rafi—what happened!" I say, reaching out to grab his arm and stop him falling.

He lowers himself slowly to the ground then closes his eyes. There is a cut just above his eyebrow, with a large lump forming underneath. His nose has been bleeding too.

"Rafi, are you OK?" I can see that he's definitely not OK.

He leans his head back against the wall and holds one hand in front of his stomach. I try to think what Mila would do when Amit and I hurt ourselves. She would clean the wound and put a dressing on it. I reach over for my sheet and tug at the end trying to rip a strip off. After a few tugs I make a small tear, then with another tug it rips like paper.

Holding three strips of sheet and my plastic water bottle I slip through the hole and run towards the platform. I don't care who sees me. I weave round passengers with boxes and bags at their feet. Some of them push me or kick at me if I get too close. In the toilet I soak the rags and fill the bottle, then head back.

Rafi is sitting in the same position. His eyes are closed but I don't think he's asleep. Every now and then he winces. I take one of the rags and wipe some of the blood from his arm. His eyes flick open and for a second he stares at me, then they close again. I clean his arms and, very gently, the side of his face below the cut. He gasps and raises his hand to his head. I throw the dirty rags in the corner. I can see a purplish colour around the bump on his head now, and another above his nose.

"Have some water," I say, placing the bottle in the hand which isn't draped over his stomach.

After a minute or so he raises it to his lips and takes a few sips. He coughs and then groans, clutching at his stomach.

I go and sit on the remains of my sheet, watching Rafi. I know it's possible to be injured on the inside, where you can't see. I wonder if that's what's happened to him. His face has relaxed and his mouth is slightly open, like he's asleep. I can see his chest rise and fall. At least he's still breathing.

What if the person who did this to Rafi watched him walking to the carriage? Maybe they saw me leave earlier too. I wasn't very careful about hiding the direction I'd come from. I sit quietly, waiting in case Rafi needs me. Watching. I'm good at waiting and watching.

Secrets

After a few hours, Rafi is still sleeping so I slip outside. I don't plan to be long. I pass kids collecting rubbish off the tracks or sitting in small groups. They are all younger than me and Rafi. The same age as Pia and Mo.

There is no one waiting outside the apartment. No sign of Dad or Amit. I try not to think about how long it is since I've seen them. It gives shape to the distance between us, and then every passing day makes my search seem more pointless.

I buy food for me, and some for Rafi. I break into my last banknote; now all I have left is a handful of coins. I must make it last.

I jump down from the edge of the platform and wait by the small trees and bushes which line the disused tracks. I walk a little further until I'm out of sight, only darting across to the empty carriage when I'm as far as possible from the station, and any curious

171

eyes. I normally only make the journey at dusk or in the dark.

Rafi is sleeping, but some of the water from the bottle has gone, so he must have had a drink. Quietly, I put a polystyrene container of rice and sauce on the floor within his reach, then I sit.

After a minute or so Rafi's eyes flicker open and he winces with pain. He looks down at the food on the floor by his hand, and then he looks over at me. The lump above his eye looks a darker colour. His hand still rests across his stomach. I realize that I'm staring at him and turn my head to look out of the window instead.

Rafi starts to talk. His voice is quiet and raspy, like he has a sore throat.

"I have a sister," he says. "I lost her too."

I say nothing. I don't want him to stop talking.

"My dad was a farmer." He speaks slowly. I can see that it hurts him. "His crops were washed away in the storms. There was nothing left for us to eat or to sell, so we came to the city. My dad was going to look for a job, but he got sick."

Rafi stops talking and looks out of the window. He sniffs, and then winces and puts his hand up to his bruised nose.

"Does my face look bad?" he asks, looking at me anxiously.

Now that he can't move his face properly, I realize how much he says with just his eyes.

"You have a big bruise on your head and a cut across your nose," I say. "But since I washed all the blood off you look a lot better."

"Thank you," he says, "for cleaning up my face."

He picks up the container of food and places it gently on his legs.

When he was talking before, it felt like he had opened a door and let me see inside a little; now I feel like it's closed again. I wait until he's had a few small mouthfuls of food.

"What happened after your dad got sick?" I ask.

He doesn't look up, but keeps eating. I don't think he's going to answer me. He finishes the last mouthful, then slowly, carefully, places the container back on the floor beside him. He looks straight at me. There's no anger in his eyes, like normal. It's like he's trying to work out something about me. Like I am a page in a book that he is trying to read.

"We had to sleep on the streets," he says, his voice still quiet. "It was hard to find a good spot. There was always someone sleeping there first. We ended up a bit further away from the other kids. I didn't usually sleep much, but I guess one night I must have, because when I woke I heard Rimi shouting out my name. Rimi is my sister. She always slept right next to me, but she wasn't there. It was dark but I could see some people pushing her into a car. I ran over but they drove off before I could get there. They took her with them."

I realize that there are tears rolling down my face. "Who took her?"

He pauses. "I didn't know, but some of the other kids saw and they said she would have to work. Probably in someone's house. They might make her do cleaning or washing or something like that. I looked for her for a long time. I went back to the place where we'd been sleeping, and walked all around there, but I didn't find her. They took her away in a car, so I guess she could be in a completely different part of the city. I used to think I wouldn't give up until I'd searched the whole city, but you can't find one person in a city this big."

He stops talking again but he's still looking at me.

I wipe my eyes and feel embarrassed that I'm crying when he's not.

"Yesterday, I thought I'd found Amit."

"What?" says Rafi. He's staring at me but not with excitement. I can't decipher his expression.

"Some little rats on the station saw a boy singing by the main road. They thought it might be him."

"Did you go?"

"Yes, I went with them. The boy wasn't Amit."

Rafi nods his head. I could be wrong, but he seems relieved. "I'm sorry," he says.

"I wondered if..." I pause, trying to find the right way to ask. "I wondered if the two little rats could sleep in here, with us."

Rafi looks up and shakes his head. It's the slightest movement, so at first I'm not sure he's saying no.

"It's a brother and sister. The girl is older and she must be about six."

"There's not enough space," Rafi says.

I look round the carriage.

"I don't want two kids to look after," he snaps. "If they come, before you know it the whole station will be sleeping here. No," he says, and I realize that's his final answer. For now.

Rafi moves his body back so that he can sit more upright, and clutches his stomach with a gasp of pain.

"What is it that hurts?" I ask.

"I don't know. My stomach or chest or maybe both." He presses his hand down gingerly. "So where is the rest of your family, Lola?"

It's the first time he's called me by my name. I wasn't sure he remembered what it was.

"My mum died when I was little," I say. It feels like such a long time since I've talked about my mum to anyone. My best friends at school know about her, but

I told them ages ago. "Dad had a factory which made clothes."

"I didn't think your family were farmers," he says. He is smiling a little bit. It's a lopsided smile, because of the bruises.

"Just after the rains got really heavy, Dad went out of town for business, and he didn't come back."

"He just didn't come back?" says Rafi.

"No. So we couldn't stay in our flat any more. The landlord made us leave."

"They threw you out? Woah." Rafi shakes his head slowly. "So rich people have bad luck too." He pauses. "But you must have somewhere else you could go, some rich friend you could stay with?"

"I thought I had a friend I could stay with. I'm not sure they want me in their house though, while I look like this."

"I thought that's what friends were for," Rafi says, "for when you're in trouble. Do you think your dad's still alive?"

His question takes me by surprise. "Yes. I wouldn't bother going to our apartment every day if I thought he was dead."

"Oh," he says, sounding guilty. He looks at me again. "Is that where you go? I wondered why you just stood outside that building for ages."

176

"You followed me?"

"I had to make sure you weren't going off to tell someone about this place." He concentrates on rubbing away a small patch of dried blood on his trousers. He places a hand on the ground either side of his hips and pushes himself up. Before he can get to his knees he gasps and clutches his stomach again.

"I think you need to rest today," I say.

"I have to go somewhere. I'm supposed to meet somebody," he says. "Stupid police," he mutters angrily.

I'm not sure I heard him right. "Why stupid police?"

"Why do you think?" he says, sounding irritated. "They're the ones who did this to me." He points to his face and body.

"What did you do?" I ask quietly. His good mood seems to be changing.

"What did *I do*?" he says, staring at me as if I might have actually arranged for it to happen. "I was sitting down," he says, "by the side of the road. That's what gets you beaten up. Not having anywhere else to sit."

"You didn't do anything wrong?"

He rolls his eyes, then winces and raises his hand to the bump. "No. We are just litter on the streets. It's like sport for them."

I think about police directing traffic, coming when there's a car accident. Then I think about the guards in the tunnel, trying to catch me. I think about the guards in the ticket hall shooing street rats away, kicking them if they get too close. Beating them.

We are both silent. I can tell that Rafi is angry, and I don't know if it's with the police, or me, or both. But he seems a lot better than this morning.

I get up and fold my sheet.

"You're going?" Rafi looks up. He doesn't look pleased that I'm going.

"I don't have much money, and I need to buy food for two people now."

He nods. I am about to lower myself through the hole when I hear a tinkling sound on the floor nearby. Rafi has placed a small pile of coins and one note on the floor. His expression is very serious.

"We can share this," he says.

"Thank you," I reply, smiling. He smiles back, his half smile. "Let's keep some money here. Then if something happens to mine, we can still eat."

Rafi raises his eyebrows then instantly groans and puts a hand to the bump on his head. "You're getting street smart," he says, sounding impressed. "I've got enough money to get by. I've got some spare too," he says.

I think about that for a second. "From carrying bags?" I ask.

"I don't really carry bags much any more. I'm an apprentice," he says quietly.

"Really? Garment work?"

Rafi's face darkens. "You ask a lot of questions. I just couldn't face carrying other people's bags any more."

"Well I'm sure they'll understand why you couldn't turn up, when they see the state you're in."

Rafi seems to calm down a little. "Yeah, maybe," he says. "Why are you always nice?"

"You let me stay here," I say, "when I had nowhere else to go."

"Yeah," he says. "Well that was just a business decision. Maybe I'm not as nice as you think."

I look at him, confused, but I can see that the door has closed again, and so have his eyes. After a few minutes he is asleep, leaning against the wall of the train carriage. I slide outside and walk down the tracks towards the platform. I can see kids playing on the lines where the trains come in and out. There is no adult to tell them to be careful.

I change direction and instead of going straight to the platform, I walk towards the scrubby bushes and trees which have grown up next to the disused tracks.

I turn a large rusty can upside down and sit. Within the bushes which grow out of the gravel and rubbish, I hear birds singing. There is a faint orange glow behind

179

the clouds. The sun must be about to set. Another layer of sound floats in on the warm air. The hum of traffic; bicycle bells ringing and horns honking.

I wonder what Amit can hear right now. He would always notice sounds or rhythms. Maybe it was the singing part of him which heard music where I didn't. I wonder whether Dad is listening to city noises too, or whether he is lying injured somewhere, and can't hear anything at all. I sit for a little bit longer, just listening.

Surprise

The next morning I wake to the sound of rain. I blink a few times and sit up. I look over at Rafi. He is on his knees, halfway to standing up. He stops and clutches his stomach before sitting slowly back down on his heels.

"I can help you," I say.

He looks up, his face tight with frustration.

"No," he says, "I don't need your help." Then, more softly, "I just need to get out of here. There are plenty of other boys like me who want to be apprentices too."

"I bet they're not all as smart as you though," I say.

He tilts his head to one side. "No one has ever called me smart," he says.

"I mean smart in the clever sense," I add, "because you definitely don't look smart in the clothes sense."

I see the small curve of a smile, before Rafi winces. The bump on his head has gone down but the dark purple colour has spread.

181

"I can't read," he says quietly. "Smart people can read."

"You could learn," I say.

Rafi looks at me. "When I was little, I wanted to learn my letters more than anything else in the world. I didn't want to be a farmer like my dad. Every year, being a farmer seemed to get harder. Maybe the crops would have some disease, or the weather wasn't right. But Dad needed me to help. So I didn't go to school. Now he's gone, and our land has gone, and I can't be a farmer either, even if I wanted to be," he says. "So I'm learning other stuff."

He puts his hand against the side of the carriage, and this time he manages to stagger to his feet. He walks slowly round the carriage a few times. Then he crouches next to the hole and lowers himself slowly down. As his feet crunch on the gravel, I hear him gasp in pain.

The rain runs from my head and down my face and the back of my T-shirt. I barely think about the journey itself, I've walked the same streets so many times. Especially now that no one seems to notice me. I am like a handrail or a rubbish bin; almost part of the street itself.

Just before I turn down my old street, I look up and see some kids in school uniforms. A group of girls in blue dresses run with their bags over their hair, squealing with laughter. A group of boys, also in blue, are running behind. I feel a twist in my stomach. The holidays must be over.

Bella and all the girls in my class will be going back to school too. They will have new uniforms and bags. They will have lots to talk about: places they've been, things they've bought. They will be learning English and biology, and maths and geography. They will have more interesting things to fill their heads than where to sleep, or how to eat.

I wonder what their new bags are like. I used to worry a lot about having the right bag. If I bought clothes, they had to be the newest label. Maybe not the ones which really suited me. If Bella asked me to suggest somewhere after school, I used to feel anxious about picking the best place to go. I felt stupid if I hadn't heard of a new film which was coming out and everybody else had. I never used to think about having somewhere safe to sleep, about going home to people who love me.

I wonder what my friends will say when I don't turn up for lessons. Maybe they will think Dad enrolled me in a school closer to home. Perhaps they will nod their heads and agree that my part of town was just too far away. If Bella knew about me coming to her house, would she tell everyone she'd seen me with my hair cut short, wearing rags like a street rat? Maybe they will try to find out from the teacher where I am, if I'm OK. I try to imagine myself sitting in the cafeteria for lunch, waiting for Bella. It feels like I was somebody else then. A completely different Lola.

I keep picturing Rafi's face when I told him why I come to the flat every day. I could tell that he thought there was no point. That Dad wasn't coming back. He made real a fear which has been swirling at the back of my mind.

There is no one outside the apartment today. Just like every other day.

I don't see Pia or Mo either. The banana man must have been there today. As I sit in the ticket hall again, I see that my world is shrinking. The other rats are trying to make a few coins or sleeping. There's nowhere to escape to. Nothing to dream for, except food and sleep.

I told Amit that we'd never be street rats. Everyone who sees me now, thinks that's what I am. Perhaps that makes it true.

When I crawl up into the carriage, Rafi is already there.

"What took you so long?" He smiles as I pull myself through the hole. It's a smile that twinkles across his whole face. I feel myself smiling back.

He's sitting with his legs crossed, his long arms in his lap. At first I thought Rafi was all bones, but he's not. He's wiry, more like an athlete.

When he keeps on staring, I hear myself saying, "What? What is it?"

Then I notice he's holding one of the sheets a little way off the ground, in front of something. With a small flourish, he whisks it aside and reveals five or six plastic containers filled with rice and different sauces. There are two pieces of flatbread and something covered in what looks like coconut. It's more food than I've eaten in the entire time since I left home.

"Where did you get all that!" I gasp.

He taps the side of his head. "My boss likes loyal apprentices," he says. "So he gave me a little extra."

"It's for both of us?" I ask.

"You helped me to get better, Doctor Lola," he says.

I'm desperate to eat something with flavour, not just bread. A wave of guilt washes away some of my excitement, as I think of Amit. The last time I ate like this was with him, watching films while we waited for Dad.

I wonder if he's as hungry as I am. What if he's eaten even less? My thoughts circle back to the fear that if I don't find him soon, perhaps he will starve.

Rafi must have noticed my smile fade.

"So there was nobody there?" he says, his mouth already half full of food.

"No. Nobody."

Rafi is still looking at me. It feels as if he can see right inside my head.

"If it makes you sad, maybe you should stop going."

I don't say anything, but I wonder if he's right. The feeling of hope on my journey there doesn't seem to make up for the sadness of finding no one there again.

"So, after your mum died, who looked after you? I mean, when your dad was working," Rafi asks.

"Mila. She started working in our home when Amit was a few days old."

"Where's Mila now?"

"She's just had a baby of her own. She lives in the slum," I say, like that's all he needs to know.

"Which slum?" Rafi asks.

"I'm not sure." I didn't realize there was more than one.

"So you've never been to her home?"

I shake my head.

I try to picture Mila in her home. In our apartment, everything about Mila was fragrant. She was the smell of washed clothes, of polished floors, of food cooking. After she'd gone home in the evening, Mila lingered in our apartment through some sweet smell within a folded T-shirt or saucepan of food. I had a few of my mother's silk scarves in my cupboard. Sometimes I would take them out and press them to my face. They didn't really have a smell, but I liked the soft feel of them against my skin.

I reach for one of the square coconut-covered cakes. I imagine the sweetness in my mouth as I hold it. "I'm so full, I'm going to save this for later," I say, and wrap it in a piece of paper.

"My stomach doesn't hurt so much," says Rafi, leaning back and pushing away the food trays.

"I guessed that by the way you were stuffing food in it. So what kind of apprenticeship are you doing?" I ask, carefully folding a second piece of paper around the cake to make it look like I'm only half-interested in the answer. "I mean, who employs someone who's falling apart like you are?"

He doesn't answer straight away, frowning instead at some spot on the carriage floor. "It's not an apprenticeship where I learn how to make furniture or mend shoes or anything," he says. "The boss has loads of people working for him."

"Does he have a big factory?" I say.

"No, it's more like he protects other people's factories."

I nod, but I don't really understand.

"He looks after some of the shops at the market, the ones which sell jewellery. But he also works for one of the rich guys on the other side of town. Does some stuff for him. He knows some of the people in the government too."

When I don't say anything, Rafi adds, "He was the first person to give me a job that wasn't carrying bags at the station. He told me that maybe one day I could be a boss too."

At first I thought Rafi didn't care what I thought. Now I realize I was wrong. It feels like he wants me to be impressed about him working for the big boss man.

"What did you want to be when you were little?" I ask. "If you didn't want to be a farmer."

"I only knew about working out in the fields. I didn't know there were other jobs I could do."

"Well, what about now?" I say. "I saw all the kids going back to school after the holidays, and it made me think about my friends being in class, studying. About all the stuff I'm missing."

"Yeah, well at least you actually *know* what you're missing," says Rafi. "I never had any school to miss." He's quiet for a minute. "I guess," he tilts his head back in thought, "I guess I'd really like to have a job where I can make something, something which I can see and touch, which I could be proud of." He runs his long fingers through his sticky-up hair and looks at me. "What did you want to do?"

For the first time it's clear in my head. I know what I wanted, only because now it's been taken away from me.

"I wanted to have a choice," I say.

"What do you mean?"

"I don't know what I want to do yet, I just know I don't want to *have* to carry bags, because that's the only choice I have."

He says, "Yeah, then maybe I was lucky I didn't have any choices. I don't know what I'm missing there, either."

"Can I come with you tomorrow?" I ask. "When you go to work."

Rafi's eyes grow wide. "No, absolutely no," he says quickly.

"I won't get in the way," I say.

"You can't come with me. My work isn't for girls," he adds.

"But I don't look like a girl any more," I reason.

"Not from a distance, maybe," says Rafi. He looks at me, and I feel the skin on my cheeks heat up. "It's not safe," he says.

"Not safe?" I reply, confused.

"I don't think you'd like all the parts of my job," he says darkly, and he starts piling up the empty food containers.

"Then..." I pause, watching Rafi look fiercely at the rubbish on the floor. "Then, do you think you could come with *me* one day?"

"Come with you where?" he snaps.

"To look for Amit. You asked me what he was wearing. You said you'd start looking out for him. It's just that, I have a feeling maybe we keep missing each other. If I go down one street, maybe he's just ahead of me, or just behind. What if we're walking round in circles together?" I almost want to smile, but Rafi scowls back.

"You don't keep missing each other," he says. "He's not there to find." I look at him sharply. "I mean, millions of people live in this city. If I couldn't find my sister, why should you be able to find your brother?

"Aren't you going to clear up?" he says, without looking up.

Gift

I wake to an empty carriage. Empty except for sheets and blankets and my small paper parcel in the corner.

I pull my trainers on and, holding the parcel gently in one hand, slide down through the hole to the gravel beneath.

Early morning travellers walk faster than passengers at other times of day, and the ticket hall buzzes with the clipping of shoes across the hard floor. I glance around at the rats gathered near the walls, hoping to spot Pia and Mo before they leave for the banana man. There's no sign of them, so I carry on towards the footpath tunnel where I spent my second night. Some rats are still packing up layers of paper, others are sitting, dazed by the morning light.

Just before I reach the other side, I see two small shapes curled up on a single piece of cardboard. I walk over and sit quietly next to them. After a few minutes,

Pia opens her eyes. She looks at me blankly, then blinks and smiles. She taps Mo on the shoulder.

"Lola is here," she whispers, like she's sharing a secret.

As Mo sits up, I pass them the paper parcel. Pia opens it and looks up at me.

"Coconut," I say, then I realize she wants to know if it's a gift. "For you to share."

Carefully, she breaks it in half and gives one piece to Mo. They bite into the cake, smiling at each other. Mo looks thinner than last time I saw him, with dark patches under his eyes.

"I thought you had a special place to sleep?" I say. "I was coming to see if I could find you. But you slept here last night?"

"Mo wasn't feeling well," says Pia. "It's warmer in here."

I think about the carriage. It's never cold in there. If Rafi is in a good mood later, I'll ask him again.

They concentrate entirely on their pieces of cake until every crumb has gone. Mo wipes his mouth then curls up on the cardboard and closes his eyes.

Pia shakes his foot. "Come on! The banana man won't have anything left for us."

"My head hurts. I want to stay here."

Pia looks at me for help. "Mo," I say, "have you ever been to work by Lola-bus?" He opens his eyes. "It's very fast and doesn't get stuck in traffic." Pia giggles. "Do you want to try the Lola-bus?"

Mo sits up and nods his head.

I crouch down in front of him. "OK, climb aboard." Mo climbs onto my back. He weighs the same as my rucksack. I feel his small hands grip my shoulders. "Pia, could you please lead the Lola-bus to Banana Man?"

Now Pia and Mo both start to giggle. I follow Pia to the end of the tunnel and up onto the main road. She walks away from the station, zigzagging down a couple of small roads until I see stalls with fruit and vegetables lining a wider street up ahead. Before we reach them, Pia stops.

"The banana man only gives the bunches to the little ones like us," she says awkwardly. "He says that he doesn't trust the older rats."

I look at Pia, trying to work out what she means.

"Oh! This is where the Lola-bus stops?"

She smiles. "Yes, this is our bus stop."

I bend down so that Mo can slide the short distance from my back to the ground. He takes Pia's hand and they walk towards the market together. As they get closer to the stalls, I half expect a mother or father to walk over and shepherd them away, back home, for breakfast. Instead, Pia and Mo head towards a big lorry, where a man passes them down a branch of bananas and tells them where they will be working for the day.

As dusk falls, Rafi slides up through the hole a few minutes after me, carrying a small box. Even though I'm usually here first, he jumps when he sees me.

"What's in the box?" I ask.

"A present from my boss," he says.

"He's showering you with gifts!" I say.

Rafi turns the box over in his hand a few times before holding it out to me. "Maybe you should have it," he says.

I take the box and open the top. Inside, nestled in white tissue paper is a pair of black trainers. I look at Rafi.

"But I've already got trainers," I say, confused.

"I thought you might like them," he says quietly.

"I do, I mean—thank you. But I think you should keep them. You need trainers more than I do." I close the box and hold it out for Rafi. He takes the box and places it on the floor next to him. He seems lost in thought. "Aren't you going to try them on?" I ask.

"What? Yes, of course." Slowly, he opens the lid and slips one onto each foot. The laces hang down by the sides. "I've never had shoes with laces before," he says.

"Oh, let me show you how to do the knot."

I lean over and tie a simple bow, then watch him do the other one. He tries a few times before making it tight, then stands up and walks from one side of the carriage to the other. It's strange seeing Rafi with anything but bare feet.

"Let's hope he doesn't give you anything else," I say. Rafi looks up. "Well, if a brand-new pair of trainers doesn't make you happy, then what will?" I smile.

He looks back down at his feet. "You make me happy." He says it so quietly, at first I'm not sure I heard him correctly. He walks over to the hole in the floor. "I'm going for a practice walk," he says, and disappears down into the dusky night.

Lies

I open my eyes. A gentle glow lights the compartment as the sun creeps above the horizon. Rafi is in the corner, quietly brushing the dust from his trainers with the corner of a bedsheet.

I close my eyes again and stay absolutely still. I hear him leave, and then wait for a few breaths until the carriage is silent once more, then throw off my sheet. I slept with my trainers on to save time. As I crawl out from beneath the carriages, I see that Rafi has already reached the platform. If he wasn't injured, I'd have no chance of catching him. Despite the bruising, he still seems to glide along the platform.

A few kids wave, or signal with their hands as Rafi passes. When he crosses the road beyond the station, I try to focus on his orange trousers. They are easy to spot as he picks a route along the edge of the road, dodging round men arranging the contents of their shops, and the rickshaws lined up at the side of the road. I barely pay attention to where we're heading.

After maybe ten or twenty minutes, I see bright colours up ahead. A row of stalls selling clothes and scarves leads into a maze of smaller passageways clogged with tables covered in bags and shoes. It looks like we've reached the edge of a market. When I shopped, it was always in a mall.

Rafi weaves between the early morning shoppers. As he walks further in, the aisles begin to narrow and I find it hard to keep him in sight. People wander in my path, and pots and piles of plastic boxes hang like bulky curtains from the stalls. I can't see the orange trousers any more. Standing on tiptoes, I peer ahead, then walk on slowly, checking left and right down the aisles off to the sides. He's disappeared.

I'm surprised by how disappointed I feel. I guess I won't find out more about secret Rafi and secret Rafi's job today. I decide to walk among the shops and stalls instead, looking at what other people can afford to buy. Stuff I didn't think twice about owning a few months ago.

I haven't gone far, when a loud voice behind me says, "Go on! Go!" As I turn, a woman pushes me angrily to the ground. "Away from here! Go away, street rat, stealing from my stall!" she says, her eyes wide.

I'm about to say that I wasn't stealing, when other stall owners come out to see what's going on. They are staring at me in the same way as the woman. I get up and walk back the way I came, without turning round.

As I reach the stalls near the road again, I smell food. Opposite, there is a small cart with pans on top. A man is cooking small pastry dumplings. Lots of people are standing around, eating breakfast from paper wrappers before heading to work. I feel safer here with a crowd. Less conspicuous.

I walk over to the stall, and before the owner can shoo me away, I hold out a coin to show that I can pay. He wraps up my food and leaves it next to the largest pan, for me to pick up. He doesn't hand it to me.

I sit on the curb, slowly tearing strips from the warm dumpling. A little further along, some ancient-looking men sit by the road with bowls in front of them. The bowls are not for food. They are for people to throw a few coins in when they pass. A thought crosses my mind, a thought which makes my mouth dry. What if I am still on the streets when I'm ancient like them?

As I finish my dumpling, above the sound of rickshaw bells and car horns, I can make out something else—a beautiful song being played nearby. I think of Amit. How many days have we been apart? How many days has he been alone? I walk towards the sound, to see who's playing the music. A little way ahead, a small crowd has gathered in front of one of the jewellery shops, their backs to me. I move closer and try to catch a glimpse of what they're looking at, but the crowd won't part for a street rat. People tut and push me away, moving closer together.

Behind me is a square lump of concrete, part of the curb which has come loose in the rains. I step up and try to balance on my tiptoes.

At the centre of the crowd, there isn't anybody playing music from a speaker. Instead, there is a child standing on a small wooden box. He is staring above the heads of the people, looking up at the sky as he sings with the pure, clear notes of a songbird. He is in tattered grey and brown clothes and wearing no shoes. His hair is thick and sticking up just like Rafi's, but I would know the curve of that nose and the outline of that face anywhere.

My brother Amit.

For a few seconds, I watch. I watch the face I thought I may never see again. It's thinner, but his voice is as beautiful as ever.

I jump down from the concrete block and run towards the crowd, trying to push my way through. Then I feel a hand on my arm. It grips tightly and I feel myself being pulled backwards. I try to tug away

200

and turn to see Rafi staring at me. I turn back to Amit, terrified to take my eyes off him for more than a few seconds, but he is obscured now by the crowd. I try to tug my arm away again.

"Stop," says Rafi. He is speaking quietly but there is an edge to his voice which makes me turn to look at him. "If you go now, that will be the end of it."

"The end of what?" I snarl, trying to pull away from Rafi's grip. I can sense that Amit is coming to the end of his song.

"Is that your brother?" he says. "Is that Amit?"

"Yes!" I say desperately. "Let me go!"

"Stop," hisses Rafi again. "You see that man standing behind your brother—the tall one?" I can just see a man's head above the crowd, near where Amit was standing on his box. He's not watching Amit like everyone else, but watching the crowd instead. "Amit belongs to him now," Rafi tells me.

I spin round. "Don't be stupid, he doesn't belong to anybody," I say, my voice getting louder. I start pulling away again, trying to reach the edge of the crowd. I feel arms round me, pinning my arms to my sides. "Let go!"

People are beginning to turn round to see what's going on.

"Stop now," Rafi hisses, "or you will lose him for ever."

"What do you mean? What are you talking about?" I gasp, struggling against Rafi's grip.

"Your brother's singing makes a lot of money. They won't just let you take him," he says. "Don't let Amit see you. If they know someone is looking for him, they won't bring him back here again. They will take him somewhere else to sing."

I turn to look Rafi in the eyes.

"Who are *they*, what do you mean 'they'?" I say.

"You helped me, now I am helping you," he says quietly.

The singing has stopped. As people move forwards to drop money in front of Amit, Rafi pushes me in the other direction, until we are out of sight beside a market stall round the corner. My arms are no longer pinned to my sides, but Rafi won't let go of me. His face is pale and I know his stomach hurts. I feel something rise up in my chest. A sob I cannot control.

"How could you stop me when I was so close to him? They would have let him go if I'd explained who I am."

"No. No they wouldn't," says Rafi flatly.

"What if he doesn't come back here? What if I never see him again?"

"They will bring your brother back here," says Rafi. "It's a good spot. People who come to the jewellery shops have more money. He's their best performer."

I sniff. Then I look at Rafi. "What did you say?"

He stares at me like he did once before, like my face is a page in a book he's trying to understand. But there's something new in his expression. Something I haven't seen before. I think it's fear.

"I said they will bring him back here. It's a good spot."

I turn so that we are facing each other. "You knew my brother was here, didn't you? You've seen him here before. You knew, didn't you? Didn't you!" I shout.

Rafi closes his eyes. "I knew they wouldn't just let you take him. I didn't want to get your hopes up, only to ruin them again. I couldn't know it was him for sure."

I keep staring at Rafi. "You knew my brother was here, and you kept it from me. My brother, maybe the only other person in my family who's still alive."

Rafi closes his eyes again. When he opens them, they glisten, but no tears fall. "I'm sorry," he whispers. "I didn't want to lose you too."

I ignore him, trying to make sense of something else he revealed.

"You said he's their best performer. That he makes a lot of money. Who for? Who does he make the money for? Who keeps it?"

Rafi stares into some empty space beyond my shoulder, thinking. When he looks at me again, he has a different expression, like he's made a decision.

He takes a deep breath in. "The man who was standing behind Rafi works for my boss. My boss keeps the money."

I stand very still, looking at Rafi in disgust. "Your boss is a gang leader? That's what you're learning to be? Some kind of gang boss?"

"What choice do I have?" he says, in barely a whisper. "You still don't understand what it means to have no choices. How could you, when you still believe you have some?"

He pauses while a man stops beside us, resting two heavy bags on the ground. The man moves away. Rafi watches him go, then his eyes lock with mine. After a few seconds, he seems to remember where we are.

"The carriage is yours now. I won't come back," he says.

He lets go of my arm. I turn and run back towards where Amit was singing. Rafi doesn't try to stop me. The crowd has gone, and so has the wooden box. The only sign that Amit has even been there is the circle of dusty footprints next to the market.

Plan

I wander through the streets, my head whirring with questions to which there are no answers. How could Rafi not tell me that he'd seen Amit? How could Rafi work for someone who makes people beg on the street for them? How can I get Amit back? It's this last question which circles round and round.

I want to go back to the market tomorrow, take Amit by the hand and run. But part of me knows that Rafi is right. The tall man would catch us in a few strides, and then what would we do? What would he do? I hate Rafi for his secrets. I hate him even more for giving me a problem but no answer.

Rafi doesn't come back to the carriage that evening. I shove his things further into the corner, out of the way. I have no money left. I head out to the ticket hall to look for passengers who need luggage carried. Maybe because Rafi shooed them off or maybe because they can tell I'm in no mood to be pushed around, the other kids don't bother me, and I get to carry four lots of luggage. My arms ache, and not one person thanks me, but at least I can eat tomorrow.

Another day passes. Another day when Amit and I could be together. Another day when Amit will wake up without knowing that I'm alive and that I've found him. Someone I've never met has taken control of my brother, of his future. Our future. Doing nothing is unbearable. What if something happens to me, or to Amit, and he never even knows I was looking for him? I feel angry, but it's a hollow anger, because there's nothing I can do.

The next morning I wake at dawn and lie on my back, staring up through the dirty window at a tiny oblong of sky. I don't have the energy to get up.

There is a noise behind me, and I turn my head to see a figure pull itself through the hole in the floor. A figure who has made that same movement many times before.

Rafi walks over to the other side of the carriage and sits down. He looks like he hasn't slept at all.

"Just let me talk," he says. "Before you ask me to leave."

I close my eyes again.

"I was going to tell you about Amit. I know you won't believe me, but I was." He pauses, like he's waiting for a response. "The longer I left it, the harder it got."

Rafi pauses again and I sense that he is looking at me. I give no sign that I am listening, but every muscle in my body is tensed, ready for the next piece of information.

Rafi clears his throat, then carries on. "At first I wasn't completely sure it was him, not until you told me what he was wearing."

I sit up and turn to face Rafi. I feel my anger rising up, with only one place to go.

"You watched me cry! You listened to me say how much I missed my brother, how desperate I was to find him—and I'm supposed to understand that it was hard for you? How difficult it was for you to tell me the truth?"

"I didn't mean—"

"What didn't you mean? You didn't mean for me to find out? I ruined everything by following you and discovering the truth?"

"Stop it!" Rafi shouts. "You don't know everything, even though you think you do."

"What else is there to know?" I shout back.

We are both on our feet. I could reach him with my hand if I wanted to.

"You knew where Amit was and you didn't tell me. If I hadn't followed you then I would have never found out. Now I have, there's nothing I can do about it anyway." My eyes fill with tears of frustration.

I sit back down, knees raised, and rest my head on my arms.

Rafi paces up from one side of the carriage to the other a few times, then I hear him sit down opposite me. He takes a deep breath and says again, "You don't know everything."

I sniff.

"I was going to tell you. I was going to tell you that night, but there was something I had to do first. Something I had to find out." He takes another deep breath. "After you told me Amit had an audition for a film, I told my boss. I knew he would be pleased with me. My boss likes Amit. He is making lots of money. He doesn't make any trouble like most of the other kids. When he heard about the film stuff, I've never seen him so excited. He started making new plans for Amit to have auditions.

"I thought he might promote me, put me in charge of something. Instead he wanted to know how I'd found out."

He stops talking while a train screeches slowly into the station.

Then, so softly that I can barely hear, Rafi says, "I told him about you." I don't look up, but I sense that he is looking at me. "My boss said I had to get you and take you to him. Maybe you would be an amazing singer too. I didn't have a good feeling about it. One of the other boys told me that if you couldn't sing, my boss would have to get you out of the way, so that there was no reason for Amit to run off. So I told my boss you had gone, disappeared. I thought he believed me at first, but he asked again. Then a couple of nights ago I think someone tried to follow me back to the station."

I breathe in sharply.

"Lola, I know I should have told you where your brother was. I know what it feels like to miss somebody. You're the first person I've told about my sister. You're the only person I've talked to about anything, since she went.

"At first it didn't seem fair that I should lose my sister for ever, and you should find your brother after only a week. If you and Amit had each other again, I thought you wouldn't need me any more. That's when I realized I didn't want to lose you too. You've never had nothing before. I've never had anything before."

The carriage is silent, but I know Rafi is still there.

A few minutes earlier I hated him. Now I don't know what I feel.

"What was the thing you had to do?" I ask.

"What?"

"The thing you had to find out?"

"I had to find out where they're keeping Amit."

I lift my head, and our eyes meet. "Did you?"

"I talked to an apprentice who's been around for longer than me. I asked him about the kids who make money for our boss." He pauses. "He told me about a building near the old fort. He said there's a place where they keep the best street workers, the ones who make the most money. It's near the markets and tourist sites. I couldn't ask any more. He was getting suspicious."

My heart flutters. "We have to go there."

"I can't," says Rafi, shaking his head. "I know most of the guys who work on the street for my boss. They know my face. If one of them saw me there, looking around outside, they'd know something was up."

I put my head in my hands. "Then how can we ever get him back? If we can't even go to the building? We might as well try and grab him when he's singing. At least then we have a chance."

"Then you'd definitely lose him for ever," says Rafi.

I don't move.

Rafi looks at me, his eyes as steady and fierce as his voice. "All I know is that I'm going to help you get Amit back. Now we know where he's sleeping every night, we have a tiny chance."

"They don't know me," I say, sitting up straight.

"Who doesn't know you?" says Rafi.

"The other apprentices. They don't know me, they don't know what I look like. I can go and find the building without anyone being suspicious."

I scramble across the floor and slip down to the gravel beneath.

"Wait, you don't know where you're going!" Rafi calls.

"So tell me," I call back, knowing he will follow.

Seconds later he is by my side, picking his way across the tracks.

"This is a bad idea," he says, jogging to keep up with me. "They might think a street kid hanging round there is a good opportunity. Especially one who looks like you do."

"Like a scruffy boy?" I say.

He must sense that there's nothing he can say to make me turn back. "I'll come with you most of the way," he says. "You'll need to do the last bit on your own."

From the tracks beside us, three kids picking litter watch with interest as we hurry past.

I know roughly which way the fort is. Rafi shepherds me, silently, turning every few metres to check that I am beside him. I'm glad he doesn't talk.

After maybe twenty minutes, I can see the red stones of the fort in the distance. It seems to rise above the apartment blocks, set back from the nearest buildings, in huge grassy grounds.

"I'll wait there." Rafi points to a crumbling white building on the corner of two roads. "Look for a grey building. He said they're doing building work next door, so there might be some scaffolding or something nearby."

I nod and carry on, sensing that Rafi has dropped behind, waiting out of sight.

I walk slowly, giving myself more time to look around. Ahead on the right, I see wooden scaffolding poles rise in a chaotic pattern.

When I'm almost level with the scaffolding, a man wanders out from the building next door, sleepily scratching his head. The building has grey walls. I swivel my eyes to the pavement and keep walking. Amit's feet must have passed over these same stones. I hear the man yawning loudly behind me.

I can't just stop and go back the way I came, so I carry on past three more buildings. Just before the fourth is a narrow alleyway. I turn down the alleyway, like that's where I'd been planning to go, and find myself emerging onto a pathway parallel to the street. Now I'm able to see the back of the grey office block. It's tall and narrow. There are three rows of windows but even the first row is far from the ground. They all have bars.

As I get closer, a flutter of excitement grows in my chest. Snaking up the walls are three fat, white drainpipes. Halfway up there is also a narrow ledge, the same grey stone as the walls.

I turn to walk back the way I came when a small face appears between the bars. The face of a child much younger than Amit. I smile up, and the child disappears out of sight.

I retrace my steps to the street, where the sleepy man is now sitting on the pavement. He stares at me as I pass. When I reach the corner where I left Rafi, he's not there. I spin round in a circle. While I'm staring at the crumbling white wall he seems to emerge from within the bricks. I step closer and see a small opening at an oblique angle, maybe where another building used to connect. In a few paces he is by my side.

We walk in silence until we're a few hundred metres away, then Rafi turns round to scan the street behind.

"What did you see?" he asks nervously.

"A man was sitting outside, so I couldn't look properly at the front of the building, but I found a way round to the back."

Rafi is looking at me intently.

"The windows are high up and they have bars, but there are drainpipes and a ledge at the back of the building."

"How far apart are the bars?" Rafi asks.

"Maybe a bit wider than my head."

He nods. We walk in silence again, Rafi lost in thought.

When we reach the station, I stop to buy bread and hand a piece to Rafi.

"For me?" His expression is deadly serious.

"For you."

His eyes twinkle.

We sit on the edge of the platform, watching some kids playing on the tracks. They can't be more than four or five years old.

We eat in silence for a minute.

"So what do you think?" I ask. I can't bear to wait any longer. "Can we get him?"

"We'll break in," says Rafi. "We don't have any other choice. We can't get a message to Amit. We don't even know which room he sleeps in."

"But I can't climb up a building."

Rafi doesn't say anything. I can sense he is thinking it over.

"Would you trust me to try?"

"What if someone from your gang sees you? They'll recognize you and then you might not even have a chance to look for Amit."

"I could say I'd been sent there to help. That might confuse them for a few minutes. Anyway, there's no reason why they should even know I'm there. We'll go at night. The darkness will be to our advantage, not theirs. I think it might be possible to climb up to one of the windows if we had some rope. We'd need the rope to get down again too. We just have to hope that I can fit between the window bars." He pauses. "There's something I haven't thought about."

"What?" I say.

"Amit doesn't know me. Why would he come with me when I'm just another stranger?"

I hadn't thought of that either.

"I know," I say, "I can tell you something that only Amit and I would know. Then he'll realize that I must have sent you."

Rafi nods.

"When can we go? How soon?"

He twists his mouth to one side. "Lola, you know that after this, whether we get Amit out or not, my boss will be out to get me. He'll know I had something to do with it. He'll be looking for me. We'll need to go to another part of the city." He looks at his feet. "I mean, I would need to. Do you think... Do you think you and Amit would come with me?" Rafi says quickly. "I thought, well, I had an idea that we could look for somewhere together. Three of us might even be able to afford a place in the slum. It would be safer there, with no guards or police to beat us, and no one to move us out." Rafi shoots me an anxious look.

"I would like us to stick together," I say. "That would be better."

A place in the slum, the three of us, is not something I could have imagined feeling good about when I was the old Lola. I would have laughed at such an awful idea. Now it seems sensible; it feels like a goal to reach.

I think about leaving this part of town. Moving away from our apartment. I think about leaving my old life behind, for good. Without Dad. Without school and my old friends. I will need something else to fill the space, something to stop me from wondering what happened. Something to stop me from thinking about Dad.

"Maybe if we had somewhere like that to stay, then one of us could go to school for a few days a week?" I say.

"Maybe," says Rafi. "As long as we were making enough to keep the room." He gives me a smile, but this time it's just his mouth, not his eyes which smile. I realize that school *and* a place to stay won't be possible.

"Lola. I was sure you wouldn't ever want to see me again," Rafi says.

"So was I," I admit. "But I've had enough of not seeing people again."

"Thank you for giving me a second chance."

Rafi jumps up.

"Oh no! I've just remembered, my boss said he had a job for me this afternoon. If there's time, I'll try and get some rope afterwards. Then I think we should go, as soon as the full moon has passed."

Rafi gives me a shy wave as he runs down the platform. I wave back, then get slowly to my feet. An intercity train is due soon, and I want to make sure I'm in the ticket hall ready to carry bags.

Escape

As dusk approaches, I think about Amit singing at the market. About how he must be wondering where I am, and why no one has come for him.

The last sleeper train pulls away from the station, rattling drowsily along the track. Rafi is late tonight. The moon rises slowly, pushing a pale oblong of light across the carriage floor. As it reaches the middle of the room, a slim figure glides up through the floor.

Rafi is out of breath.

"We have to go," he gasps, sitting with his legs still in the hole. "We have to go right now," he repeats between breaths.

"Go where?" An icy wave slides down my spine. "What's happened?" I ask.

"My boss asked about you again. Someone told him they saw me walking along with a girl. Now my boss thinks something is going on. My friend warned me. He said they might move Amit somewhere else. A different part of town. My friend took my trainers for the information."

"But without any rope, how will you get up? How will Amit get down?"

"I don't know," Rafi says. "But we can't wait another day. Are you ready?" he asks quietly. "Shall we go?"

I nod calmly. I don't feel calm.

From the sidings, we peer along the platform, but there are no guards beneath the neon lights. My trainers make a faint scuffing sound on the hard floor. Rafi's bare feet are silent.

We walk more quickly than during the daytime. There are fewer cars and people to dodge. Rafi doesn't speak, and I don't want to break the silence, in case he suddenly says that what we're doing is crazy, we'll get caught, and there's no way we can get Amit back.

When we reach the corner next to the crumbling white building where I left Rafi before, he waves at me to stop. We look down the street towards the scaffolding. I can make out a few figures walking along, but no one waiting outside the grey building. We carry on, past the front door, which is shut. I can see no lights on in any of the windows.

Amit is so close.

We turn down the narrow alleyway which leads to the back of the buildings. I wait, motionless, as

Rafi looks up towards the ledge, working out how to reach it.

He turns to me and whispers: "You will have to come up too. Then if something happens to me, you can show Amit how to get down."

Before I can say no, silently, he places one hand on either side of the drainpipe and slides his right foot up, then his left foot, like he's climbing the trunk of a coconut tree. He reaches the ledge in less than a minute, then beckons to me.

I take a deep breath and rub my hands together, then copy what Rafi did, but my feet keep sliding on the plastic. Rafi is waving at me to hurry up. I untie my laces and slip my trainers off as quietly as I can. My bare feet can grip much better.

I move up slowly. The muscles in my arms begin to burn. When my head is level with the ledge, I reach an arm up to grab it, but instead feel myself tipping backwards. Rafi reaches down and grasps my wrist, then pulls me in towards the building. While he holds me, I am able to swing one leg over the ledge, then the other.

He puts his finger to his lips and pauses to listen for noises from inside, then grips the bottom of the window frame and in a single motion vaults inside, sliding feet first through the gap between the window bars. It's just like the hole into our train carriage, only five metres above a solid concrete path.

Now I strain to hear any sound from inside. It's eerily quiet. I get slowly to my feet and grab the thin metal window bars, being careful not to look down. I feel safer now that I have something solid to hold on to.

Inside, a yellowish glow filters through a doorway, casting a pale light across the dark room. The floor looks uneven, covered in something. Rafi picks his way slowly towards the door.

"Amit," he whispers. "Is Amit here?"

My eyes begin to adjust and I realize that the uneven floor is actually rows of children lying asleep. The floor rustles and shifts and I see a small figure sit up. I feel my heart beating in my chest. The figure points to the doorway, and Rafi creeps towards it, keeping low. More children sit up and whisper to each other.

A few minutes later Rafi reappears silhouetted, next to a smaller shape.

"Amit! Amit!" I whisper.

A murmur begins to spread around the room as children point over at me.

The smaller shape peels away from Rafi, stumbling above legs and heads to reach me. Moonlight catches the figure's face.

"Lola!" Amit says. He grips the window bars. I reach my arms between them and pull Amit towards me. I feel his head on my shoulder, his breath on my arm as I squeeze him tight. He looks up. "What happened to your hair?" he says, shocked.

"Fashion," I answer quickly.

Behind, Rafi is waving his arms at us to go. He is standing just outside the room, looking left and right.

Amit is more agile than me and in a second his feet are through the hole. I move to the side and let him slide down, feet first.

"Slowly," I say, "the ledge is narrow."

The other boys in the room begin to whisper more loudly. "Amit, where are you going? Who is that?"

His toes reach the ledge and I take his arm to steady him so that he can sit down.

As soon as Amit is through, Rafi rushes to join us. He puts his hands on the window bars, ready to jump.

"Who's there?" a deep voice shouts.

Rafi lets go of the bars and turns in the direction of the voice. A figure fills the doorway. Rafi runs back through the sitting children. I see him try to shut the door but the man on the other side is stronger, pushing back, forcing it open.

Amit begins to stand so that he can see what's going on. I shake my head.

"Amit, we have to get down as fast as we can." I point to where the drainpipe meets the ledge. "Hold onto the ledge until you've gripped the drainpipe with your feet."

"Me first?" he whispers.

"Wait for me at the bottom," I say. I look back through the window. Rafi is grappling on the floor with the man. There are shouts from further inside the building.

The children have moved to the sides of the room. Some are looking at the figures rolling on the floor, some are looking through the window at me.

Amit clings to the top of the drainpipe, sliding his feet carefully down. He's fast, like Rafi.

I sit with my feet hanging over the ledge, then turn round slowly to lower myself down. I feel for the drainpipe with my feet but I don't want to let go of the ledge. It feels like I'll fall backwards again.

"Don't worry," I hear Amit say from somewhere underneath me, "it's not far."

From inside the room the shouts are getting louder.

I reach down and grab the drainpipe with one hand, then the other. I cling on for a few seconds, then start to slide myself down. When I'm a few metres from the ground, I lose my grip and push myself away from the wall, landing on the concrete beneath, my legs buckling.

Amit is next to me in seconds.

"Are you OK?" He bends down and takes my hand. The skin has come away from my palms, and my knees hurt. He pulls me up.

"Stop!" A man's face looks down at us from the window above.

I look at Amit. "Ready to run?" I ask. He nods. "Follow me and don't look back."

I don't head towards the alleyway. Instead I run in the opposite direction, along the path behind the buildings. Stones press sharply into the soles of my feet. I realize that now, without my shoes, I am completely street rat.

Amit runs beside me. He has no trouble keeping up. After a few minutes, we reach a metal fence. It has straight bars with pointed tops which aren't sharp. Amit clambers up and jumps over then turns to offer me his hand. I clamber up then grip his hand before jumping down. I can't help looking behind. No one is following us. Not the man, not Rafi either. We have landed on grass which means we must be in the grounds of the fort.

"We have to keep going," I gasp.

We run to the far side of the grounds, where the grass meets a road. There are no lights here so we should be hard to spot.

"Let's stop for a minute to catch our breath," I say, leaning forwards, with my hands on my bruised knees, my chest heaving.

Amit sits down on the grass. After a minute or so, he says quietly, "I thought I'd never see you again."

"Sometimes I thought the same thing," I say. "But I never stopped looking."

"How did you find me?"

"Rafi. The boy who came to get you. He found out where you were. I saw you singing at the market too. But I couldn't just come and get you. Rafi told me they wouldn't let you go."

"Where do you think Rafi is now? Do you think he got away?"

"Rafi always turns up. He's like a cat with nine lives." As I say the words I realize that he must have used up most of them by now. "We should get going."

"Where to?"

"To the place where I agreed to meet Rafi. No one knows about it except us."

Amit

Amit has no trouble pulling himself up into the carriage, nothing like me the first time I tried. We sit close together, our knees almost touching. He looks around the space.

"This is where you've been staying?"

"Mostly," I say. "When I wasn't looking for you."

Amit nods. "The day I lost you, I looked for you in the crowd for so long. Then I waited by the side of the road. I didn't know where I was. I waited all day. When you didn't come, I didn't know what to do. I was so hungry."

Amit starts to cry. I put my arms round him. He sniffs and wipes his nose, then carries on talking.

"I think it was the next day when some kids saw me on my own and told me I should go with them. I followed them until we got to a market. They were taking things from people's bags and they wanted me to do it too, but I didn't want to.

"I wandered around for a bit near the food stalls, waiting to see if there might be something I could eat. An old man was singing there. I think he was blind. People were dropping coins onto a piece of card in front of him, so I went and started singing with him. Soon there was a big crowd of people. When the old man stopped singing, I stopped too. He gave me a coin to buy something to eat."

He pauses to wipe his nose again.

"While I was eating, a woman came over and said she'd heard me singing and that she could help me. She told me I was lucky she'd found me before anyone else had, and she would look after me. I wasn't sure whether I should trust her, but I didn't have anywhere else to go.

"She took me to the place you saw. At first it felt OK—better than being on my own on the street. After a few days, though, I realized that I was being treated better than the other boys. I was hungry, but they had even less to eat than me. We would get up early every day and go to different places so that I could sing. I'm not sure what the others did.

"Back in the room there was nothing to do except sleep, but we were out for most of the day anyway. I didn't see the lady much again. Sometimes the boys would disappear and no one knew where they went.

The men told us they had found homes for them, but I didn't believe that. I was worried they might find a 'home' for me."

I listen, nodding to encourage Amit, but he doesn't need it. He wants to talk. The distance between us dissolves as his words wash through the empty spaces left by endless questions, replacing them with real places and events.

I tell Amit about finding Rafi in the train, and about how I looked for Amit and Dad every day. I leave out the bits about being chased by the guard, and Rafi being beaten up. I have a feeling Amit left out some bits too.

As evening comes, Rafi hasn't returned.

"Do you think they're keeping him prisoner?" says Amit. "What should we do?"

I think for a minute. "Maybe they *are* keeping him prisoner. I don't know. It would be crazy to head back to where you were staying, but I can't just sit here any longer. Something is wrong." I know what I have to do. "Amit, I'm going to retrace the route I took with him and look for clues."

I don't have any better ideas. I don't want to take my brother with me, in case someone from Rafi's gang spots us, but I cannot bear to leave him behind.

I rummage around in Rafi's pile of sheets, looking for a different T-shirt for him to wear. There is a grey one which is full of holes. There is also a green sheet. I tug it away from the pile.

"Amit, come over here," I say. "Put your arms out." He stands patiently with his arms raised as I wrap the sheet round him, finally draping it loosely over his head.

I smile. "No one will be looking for an eight-year-old girl." Amit looks unsure. "If you go out like this then no one will recognize you, it's the perfect disguise."

He puts his hands up to touch the fabric draping down from his head. "OK." He nods, tilting his head to one side. He is getting into character already.

Rescue

We set off as the daylight begins to fade, replaced by patches of neon glow. A light rain is falling. As we head away from the station, Amit and I peer in the dark corners and side streets. I feel like an expert in looking for people. Not in finding them, perhaps. When we reach the junction by the white building, I decide it's too risky to go any further.

"Maybe we can come back in the morning and look again?" Amit says.

As we turn to go, I see something move on the wall opposite. I remember the hollow where Rafi waited for me.

I walk closer and see a pair of legs stretched out across the width of the gap. Rafi is propped against the wall, clutching one arm with the other.

"Rafi," I whisper.

As I walk closer, Amit is right behind me. Rafi's eyes flicker open and he looks down at his arm.

"I can't move it," he whispers back. "It hurts too much."

"Can you walk?" I ask.

"I hurt my ankle too," he says.

I take a step back and scan left and right to see if anyone is coming. We need to get away from here. One of Rafi's gang could come out of the grey building at any moment, and see us. If Rafi can't walk, then we will have to carry him, but I don't see how we can lift him under his damaged arm.

"Amit, I think we're going to need your sheet," I say.

Rafi doesn't even look up while I help Amit remove his disguise and lay it on the ground next to him.

"Can you take his legs?"

Amit lifts Rafi's legs just above his ankles, and I put my arms round his waist and slide him out from the hollow. Rafi whimpers with pain.

We place him down gently in the middle of the sheet. He's not very heavy. I gather up the spare fabric spread out above Rafi's head. Amit does the same by his feet. Rafi is wrapped up like a boy-sized sweet.

"Are you ready?" I ask Amit. He nods.

Gently, we lift Rafi from the floor and begin to walk back to the station, Rafi hanging between us. I hear him groan quietly from within the sheet.

I scan around for anyone taking an interest in Amit, now that he has no disguise, but people are more interested in our strange luggage. I try not to meet anyone's gaze.

When we reach the station, it's night-time. At the end of the platform we lay Rafi near the edge, so that we can jump down onto the track. My arms ache as we carry him the final few metres, then put him gently down on the ground next to the train.

"Do you think you can make it inside the carriage?" I ask him.

He shakes his head.

I gather all the sheets from his special corner and place them in layers over the gravel. Rafi manages to lie on top of them, groaning in pain whenever something moves or touches his arm. Below his elbow is a large bump, and it looks as if the bone has broken.

Rafi seems different to the last time he hurt himself. He's not fighting to get better. Amit and I fetch him water and food, and then Amit climbs inside the carriage for a rest.

I sit down next to Rafi. He stares over at me from his bed of sheets.

"How did you get away?" I ask softly.

"Through the front door. There were only two guys guarding the kids. After you'd gone they were too busy trying to stop some of the other kids escaping through the window."

"Did they recognize you?" I ask.

"One of them did," Rafi says quietly. "And now my arm is all broken up."

"Your arm will get better," I say. "Bones can heal."

"I've seen street kids who broke arms or legs. They never heal right. They're never able to use them properly afterwards. How can I carry things now? How can I do anything?"

Tears roll down his face, leaving trails on his dusty skin. I've never seen Rafi cry.

"We'll find somewhere new to stay. Somewhere in the slum, where we can be together, safer. Just like you said."

"Well, that was before. Now we'd never have enough money. Not with me to look after as well."

"Your arm hurts," I say, "and you haven't eaten anything. You'll feel much better when you have, and when you've slept for a bit."

"I'm so glad you got your brother back, Doctor Lola." Rafi smiles, but it's a small smile, not one of his brilliant, twinkling ones.

"I never would have without you," I say.

"You nearly didn't because of me," he replies.

"Well, good job I was sneaky enough to follow you to work."

After a while his eyes close, and I climb inside the carriage to get some sleep.

Paper

In the morning, I wake and see Amit sleeping on the floor next to me. A smile creeps across my face.

His eyes open and he sits up, running his hands through his spiky hair. "Wow, I haven't got up this late in a long, long time." He laughs. "I might not do any singing today. I'm hungry," he adds.

All the things which used to annoy me about Amit are all the things I missed too.

"I think Rafi has a bit of money we can borrow for food. We can't risk trying to make any money in this part of town though. Rafi's gang will be looking for us."

"So will we have to leave here?"

"As soon as Rafi can walk, we'll need to go a long way from this part of town. Maybe a different city."

Amit freezes. "Leave the city? But what about Dad? We can't leave without him."

"If Rafi's boss finds us, he'll take you back, and he'll punish Rafi. Maybe me too."

"When did you last go to our apartment?" Amit asks.

"I'm not sure. Maybe three or four days ago," I reply.

"Can we go there today?" he says. "I want to have a look too."

I lower myself down to where Rafi is lying. His eyes are open.

"Rafi," I whisper, "I think Amit and I are going to our old apartment," I say. "Together."

"OK," says Rafi. "Be careful." He smiles, but it doesn't reach his eyes. "Amit should wear something different. He'll be harder to recognize."

As we turn the corner to our street, I take Amit's hand. We walk along together, to the front of our apartment building. After everything we have been through, the building looks bizarrely unchanged. Stubbornly silent. It doesn't feel like home any more.

Amit bends down to pick up a marigold flower from the floor. The only one left intact from a chain of blossom. A gentle breeze twists along the street, and I tilt my chin up to feel the cool air across my face. An old poster flaps on the telegraph pole like a dirty flag.

I tug at Amit's hand to start walking again, but he pulls away, stopping in front of the poster. He doesn't move. I walk over to see what he's looking at. He rips the paper from the pole and presses it into my hand. The paper is torn and the writing blurred by rainwater.

At the top I can just make out the word *Lost*. I look more closely. The next word I see is halfway down. It looks like *Lola*. There is some more writing I cannot read. At the bottom is a phone number. I stare at it, just like Amit did seconds before. Lola isn't a very common name in our city. How many times have I walked past this piece of paper before and not seen it? I only ever look at the building.

With my heart racing, I grab Amit's hand; in the other hand I hold the piece of paper. We run down the street together to find someone who will let us use their phone.

The first shop we see sells bags of rice. As we enter, a man appears from somewhere near the back and shoos us out before I even open my mouth, clapping his hands like he is trying to scare a stray cat or dog.

Next door is a fabric shop. The owner listens to me first before shaking his head and waving us away. Maybe he is worried we will run off with his phone. I hear the *tink, tink* of a hammer and chisel from a shop selling bracelets carved from shells.

"Amit, why don't you try this time? Maybe it's better if I wait outside."

Amit walks into the shop and approaches a man sitting behind a desk covered in tools and bits of shell. He listens to Amit, then takes the piece of paper. A thrill of fear runs through my chest as he holds the most precious thing we have casually between two fingers.

He picks up his phone and dials a number. After talking for a few seconds, he passes the phone to Amit. I want to go in, but don't dare in case the spell is broken and the man snatches back his phone.

When Amit has finished talking, the man takes his phone and gives Amit the paper and something else, which I can't see. Amit turns round and I see that he is crying. I stop breathing.

As he walks towards me, I hear myself saying, "What is it? What happened?"

"He's coming for us."

I stare at Amit for a moment. His eyes are shining with tears, and with happiness. I throw my arms round him and we stand in the doorway like that, until the man tells us to move out because we're blocking the way for other customers.

"He said he would come to the apartment."

I take Amit's hand and we run back up the street, dodging shoppers and rickshaws.

We sit on the curb and wait.

I cannot let myself picture Dad's face. After so much disappointment, I can't quite believe I might be about to see it again.

Dad

I stare along the road until my eyes feel dry. A man and woman appear round the corner, each carrying a box. Then a man, younger than Dad, walks past on his mobile phone.

Next, I see a figure walk slowly round the corner and stop. My heart thumps. The figure begins to move again. A man. He has a bad limp and one arm hangs by his side.

I look at Amit. We scrabble to our feet and start running towards the figure.

The man stops and watches us approach. I see him blink a few times, and then begin to smile, first around his eyes, then his whole face crinkles.

He holds out one of his arms and wraps it round my shoulder. Amit clings to his side, where the other arm hangs down.

"Dad," I whisper. "You're alive."

"I am so sorry, Lola," he whispers back.

I expected Dad to look like he did the night he left. He is much thinner.

All the tears, all the sadness of the last weeks can't stay locked away any more. I lean against Dad as my shoulders heave up and down.

"I thought you were dead," I sob into his shirt.

"So did I, Lola, so did I."

I don't know how long the three of us stand there like that, before Dad says, "You both look like you need something to eat."

We walk slowly down the street and into the first place we find. We order food and huddle round a table near the back.

"I think short hair rather suits you," says Dad. "I also think you were very clever to cut it short. Amit, your hair looks completely unchanged." He ruffles the top of it and a few pieces of grit fall onto the table.

"Dad," I say. He looks down at the table, the way he used to look down at his paperwork when I asked questions about Mila leaving. "Dad, what happened? Where have you been?"

He breathes in slowly, then begins to talk.

"I knew I shouldn't leave town that weekend. The rains were bad, especially where I was going to. I decided to make the journey there and back in one day, which was another bad decision. I arrived late, and only just had time for my meeting.

"When I left the city, late in the afternoon, it was raining so hard I could barely see where the road was. There was water all around. The fields were flooded, so I didn't notice at first that a river had burst its banks and was starting to flow over the highway. Suddenly I couldn't steer the car any more, it was being swept along. There were many other cars too, and trucks. None of us could get out. We would have drowned.

"Lots of cars were being pushed towards a steep bank at the side of the road. The water had found a place to flow down to some lower fields. I remember my car drifting towards the bank. I don't remember anything after that."

I realize that I've been holding the same piece of food the whole time Dad has been talking. I put it back on my plate. Dad seems tired and stops talking to take a sip of tea. Amit pushes his chair right up close to Dad's, so that their arms are touching.

"I woke up in hospital, and I couldn't really move. I didn't know what had happened. The doctor told me I had broken some ribs and crushed a nerve in my arm. My leg was badly bruised. I had concussion." He looks at Amit. "A nasty bang to my head. They said I'd been there three or four days. They didn't know who

I was. My phone and my wallet with my ID had all been washed away.

"For a little while, I couldn't remember either. My head was very sore. After a couple more days, my memories began to return. Then all I could think about was you two, alone. I was one of the lucky ones. Hundreds of people died that weekend."

Dad stops to sip some more tea. Amit cannot take his eyes off Dad; he has barely eaten anything either.

"After another week, I left the hospital. They said I should stay longer, but I couldn't bear not knowing what had happened to you both. When I arrived at the flat, the guard wouldn't let me into the building. He wouldn't take a note for you either. That's how I found out you'd gone."

Dad sniffs and looks up to the ceiling.

"I've been so stupid," he says. "I nearly lost the two things I care most about in the world."

Amit and I look at each other.

"What do you mean?" Amit says.

"I mean, what has happened is all my fault," says Dad.

"But you didn't know the river would burst its banks. How can it be your fault?" I ask.

My dad puts his head in his hands. He stays like that for a minute or so. I start to wonder if he's OK.

"Dad?" Amit puts his hand on his shoulder.

242

"I went because I had to get a new order for the factory. The factory isn't making as much money as it used to."

"I thought it was getting bigger?" says Amit.

"There are more staff, but fewer orders. The big international companies are taking all the business, but they don't pay enough for me to subcontract their projects."

"But we moved into a bigger flat," I say. "I thought the factory was doing well."

My father frowns. "Not well enough."

"So why did we move?" I ask.

Dad gives a gentle laugh.

"Because I felt ashamed about you having to sit in the traffic for hours, about not living closer to the school and to your friends. Of not having a driver. I felt ashamed that I couldn't give you those things."

"I thought you didn't like the part of town they lived in? You said it was overpriced."

"Yes, that's true." Dad smiles, mostly in his eyes. "But it is also true that we couldn't have moved there anyway. I thought moving to a bigger flat would make it better. Then we lost another big order at the factory, and I couldn't pay the rent. I was a fool."

I don't like Dad calling himself a fool. "But you were only trying to make things nice for us," I say, feeling a pang of guilt when I remember complaining about living in the old town.

243

"I took a stupid risk. I let money stop me from remembering what is really important. That is something worth feeling ashamed of." Then Dad adds quietly, "Of all people, I should remember that family is more important than wealth."

Amit frowns, confused. "Why?" It's the question I also wanted to ask.

Before Dad can answer, a man comes to our table and asks if we would like to order anything else. Dad shakes his head. "We have enough, thank you." He turns back to us. "Come on, eat up."

"So where will we live now?" Amit asks, lifting a chip to his mouth. "Will we still have no home?"

"I have a few savings, which I will use to pay the landlord. But it will take a while to get back on our feet. I've been to the factory and we can start production again soon, but we need time to get going properly. Yesterday I found a flat not far from here. It's small, but we can fit. We won't be on the streets, but things will be different for us now. There won't be any money to spare."

"Does that mean I don't have to go to school any more?" Amit says, grinning.

"No," says Dad, sounding like himself again. "It does not mean that. Oh, I almost forgot. I have something for you," Dad says, holding out a small paper package. "I thought that as I've been away for longer than usual, you might like something more than marigolds." He looks at me, his eyes twinkling their familiar twinkle.

Inside the blue paper is a thin gold bracelet. It is precious, and beautiful. I slide it over my hand and hold my arm out. It looks out of place against my grubby clothes. "Thank you, Dad, I love it."

"I wasn't sure it would suit you," Dad teases Amit.

"I have something already," says Amit. He shows me a smooth creamy-coloured disk with something carved on it. "It's a shell," says Amit. "The man said I could keep it. He said maybe it would bring me luck, and our family would be together again."

"You two need to finish, then I can take you to the apartment. It isn't far, but my leg is still healing."

I start eating slowly.

With a wave of guilt, I think of Rafi, lying beneath the train carriage on his own. I put down my piece of bread.

"Dad," I say, "I can't go straight to the apartment."

"Why not?" says Dad.

"I have to help my friend."

"He's hurt himself," says Amit.

"Who is your friend?" says Dad.

"Somebody who helped me. He gave me somewhere to stay, and he helped Amit too. But now he's in trouble. He doesn't have anyone else. He's called Rafi."

"Where is he?" asks Dad.

"He's at the train station. I think we might need to take him to a hospital."

Dad holds his hand up to get the waiter's attention. "We will take a taxi to the station instead then," he says. "OK, Amit?"

Amit nods his head. "*Yes yes yes*," he sings, waving his arms in the air. It seems he didn't need a break from singing for long.

"Come on," says Dad, "let's go and get Rafi."

We flag down a taxi. It takes my dad a little while to manoeuvre his leg in through the door. The driver pulls back into the traffic, joining lines of rickshaws, taxis and small vans. As people beep their horns impatiently, I watch the street kids weaving between the cars.

Truth

I walk across the gravel towards the rusting carriages once more. This time when I turn to look at the platform, Dad and Amit are sitting at the end, waiting for me.

I get down on my hands and knees and crawl beneath the train, conscious, once more, of the dirt. I can't see Rafi or his sheets. My stomach flips as I realize he's been able to pull himself into the carriage after all. I slide myself up and through the hole.

I look around, confused. The carriage is empty.

The sheets and other things which Rafi keeps in the corner have all gone. In the middle of the floor is a small piece of folded fabric. I rush over and pick it up. It's Amit's T-shirt. The one Rafi stole.

I walk slowly back towards the end of the platform. Dad and Amit watch me with anxious expressions.

"Where is Rafi?" Dad asks.

I sit down in between them. "He's gone," I say. Tears roll down my face. "I've found you, and now I've lost him."

We sit in silence for a while, all three of us staring out across the tracks.

"I'm sorry," says Dad. "How can you be sure he's not coming back?"

"He made his boss angry when he told me where I could find Amit, so now he doesn't have a job. And he's hurt his arm so he can't carry bags either."

"But that doesn't mean he's gone away and he's not coming back," says Dad.

"It does," I reply. "I know Rafi. He said that when we found Amit, maybe we could pay for somewhere to live together, all three of us. Somewhere safer. He knows that if he can't work, he can't pay. That's why he's gone. He didn't want to get in the way."

"He sounds like a special person," my dad says, "to put others before himself."

"He is special."

"I can see there's a lot we need to talk about," says Dad. He looks so tired. "Perhaps we should go back to the flat now, while we think about what to do."

I nod.

As we leave the station I feel a little tug on my hand. I turn round and see Mo; Pia is standing just behind him.

"Can you wait a minute?" I say to Dad. He nods.

I crouch down, ignoring the crowds of people flowing either side of us.

"You look different again," says Pia.

"Cleaner," says Mo.

Pia's eyes open wide. "Where did you get that from?" She's looking at my bracelet.

"From my dad," I say, turning round to where Dad and Amit are waiting near the rickshaws. "I found my family." I slide the bracelet down over my wrist and pass it to her. Pia takes it, turning it round in her hands. "Keep it. Now you can go and find yours."

Her eyes light up. Mine fill with tears.

Pia slides the bracelet up her arm, until it's out of sight beneath the sleeve of her top. "Leave today if you can," I say. I hug them both, then I wave as they melt into the crowds, heading for the platforms.

We follow Dad through the door and into a narrow hallway. The air conditioning makes me shiver. We look around together. The flat is almost empty, and much smaller than our old apartment, but everything seems so shiny. I go into the bathroom and wash my hands.

"Why don't you have a shower?" Dad shouts.

I don't care that there is no shampoo. I rub soap over my skin and into my short hair and watch the soot and mud wash away down the plughole. I realize that I have no new clothes to wear and as I put my jeans back on, the dirt rubs off onto my clean hands.

I walk past the hall to a small room by the kitchen, where Amit is sitting on a sofa with Dad. I sit on the floor in front of them.

After a few moments, Dad says, "I've never really talked to you about why I don't keep in touch with the rest of your family. Perhaps it's time I did." He looks at me, then Amit.

"I first met your mother when I was setting up my business. She came to the factory because she wanted a job."

We stare at Dad, not wanting to miss a word. He often talked about Mum, but not like this, not about before we were born.

"Your mother's family were educated and so was she, but they fell on hard times. When I met her, they were living in a slum. I couldn't offer your mother a job."

"That's not very kind," says Amit.

"I couldn't offer your mother a job, because I fell in love with her the first time I met her. When I told my family I wanted to marry her, they were appalled. They forced me to make a choice—them, or her. I chose your mother."

"So your family didn't like Mum because she was poor?" I ask.

"Basically, yes."

"But you married Mum anyway?" I say.

"Yes." He pauses. "And if she was alive now, she would have told me how ridiculous it was to move to a bigger flat to impress people."

We sit in silence, until Amit says, "But we're together now."

"For ever," I add.

Dad closes his eyes and nods. "For ever," he says.

That night, I lie in a real bed. The mattress feels so incredibly soft. I think of Rafi lying somewhere on a piece of cardboard. I drag my sheet from the bed and lie on the floor next to it. I'm not quite ready for a real bed yet. Not while Rafi is sleeping on the streets.

Before I can go to sleep, I get up again and walk to Amit's room. I see him breathing peacefully. Then I walk to Dad's room. He looks up.

"Can't sleep either?" he says.

"Just doing a head count," I say. "Goodnight."

I lie on the floor and think about what Dad told us about Mum. They chose to be together. Money didn't matter.

I'm not sure which school I'm going back to, or when, yet, but I already know one thing for certain. Choices are precious. From now on, I'm not going to let people make my choices for me. Not Bella, not anyone.

I know that means I'll have to be a little braver, because the first choice I make is to do what feels right, even if it's not what my friends would do. I'm going to start by asking Dad where Mila lives. I want to go and see her and her new baby. Maybe I could try to make them some doughnuts. Well, not the baby.

I listen to the tinkling of bicycle bells. I know that somewhere in the city, Rafi is listening to the same sound. Rafi said you can't find one person in a city this big, but now I know that's not true. Everyone needs one person looking out for them.

I am going to be Rafi's. I won't give up on him. Ever.

Acknowledgements

The encouragement, skill and determination of so many people lie within the pages of a book. Thank you. I am so grateful for it all. Special thanks to Charlie Viney for your confidence in me. Thank you to Sarah Odedina, always. Thanks to Adam Freudenheim, and the Pushkin Children's Books team; to Rory Williamson, to India Darsley, to Tilda Johnson for tidying up so elegantly, and to Thy Bui for the beautiful cover. Thanks to Mum and Dad for always dropping everything to look after the kids – and arriving with wine. Now I've written it here, you will have to continue with that. To Lily and Scarlet for being utterly awesome, and for letting me watch Hey Duggee when I need a break. To Tim, without whom, I would still be on my millionth draft of page one (paragraph one). To the brilliant and dedicated booksellers, librarians, teachers and reviewers who champion children's books tirelessly. To children's books authors everywhere – my inspiration.

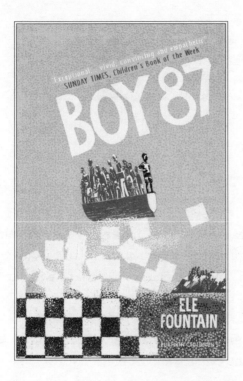

'Exceptional... vivid, convincing and empathetic... it grips us with the need to know how the heart-stopping events will turn out... a tale of our time, imparting understanding and sympathy... powerfully told, without sentimentality'

Sunday Times, Children's Book of the Week

PUSHKIN CHILDREN'S BOOKS

We created Pushkin Children's Books to share tales from different languages and cultures with younger readers, and to open the door to the wide, colourful worlds these stories offer.

From picture books and adventure stories to fairy tales and classics, and from fifty-year-old bestsellers to current huge successes abroad, the books on the Pushkin Children's list reflect the very best stories from around the world, for our most discerning readers of all: children.